Messages

For Kim
Thanks for
being here —

Susan Brown

Cover Drawing By Suzanne Johnson

Messages

New And Selected Poems
1969 - 1989
Luke Breit

Introduction By Norman Mailer

published by
Q.E.D. Press
Fort Bragg, California

Acknowledgments

Some of these poems have appeared in the following periodicals and anthologies: The New Yorker; Poet News: Sacramento's Literary Review; *The California Bicentennial Poets Anthology*; The Mendocino Commentary; The Mendocino Grapevine; The Haight Ashbury Literary Review; *Landing Signals: An Anthology of Sacramento Poets*; *Four Sacramento Poets*; Pinch Penny; and *Editors' Choice II: Fiction, Poetry & Art From The U.S. Small Press.* Except for the selection: *New Poems*, these poems are from the collections: *Celebrating America Within* (Golden Mountain Press); *Words The Air Speaks* (Wilderness Poetry Press); and *In This Picture, We Are Laughing* (WUFAHTIBOOTDA Poetry Press).

ISBN 0-936609-17-6

Published by
Q.E.D. Press
Quod Erat Demonstrandum*
155 Cypress Street
Fort Bragg, California 95437
(707) 964-9520

**That which was to have been demonstrated has been proved.*

Introduction

After months of working a lot, I had to work very hard for the last few weeks, and my body landed finally in the same place as my spirit--gridlock. My legs cramped when I stood up to walk. This stint came to an end about five days ago, and I have been trying to relax ever since. I've been drinking and going out with good people, but it's not been coming around all that well. After a day of catching up with correspondence (which, after months of writing, feels like ditch-digging), I picked up this collection by my old friend Luke Breit, started pretty much on page one, and read most of the poems. Now a couple of hours later, my inner traffic is beginning to move forward again. Luke Breit is Doctor Breit, Traffic Consultant for locked-up synapses and totally fucked-up grace. Reading his poems proved one hell of an unexpected benefit. While I knew he was good, nay, very good, since he has surprised me before by how good he is, nonetheless I had never read so many of his poems at once, and to my surprise, I think they've done what poetry is supposed to do, and even used to do until the last forty or fifty years of Western Civ began to ruin everything that curved or sagged or dripped or blew or offered you subtle shadow. Poetry used to put a little wine in your lungs with a fresh breath, and just so, I felt a little bit alive once more after reading *Messages*.

Years ago, I wrote a blurb for *Words The Air Speaks* which went like this:

> *I think Luke Breit succeeds in writing with a fine edge right into the tendrils of natural change. No one does more with a mist, or the quiet desperation of a root, no young poet I know is so successfully and consistently tender without ever embarrassing the*

reader. Luke Breit celebrates emergence
from gloom—what a nice feat. What skill in
the simplicity.

If Breit knows how to take us out of gloom, it is because he understands sorrow, particularly a lover's sorrow. He catches that place where paranoia is so sensuous it can ameliorate anguish before it has to increase it. Listen to these lines from "Things to Believe In":

Evenings she doesn't come are few but empty.
The furniture of the house belongs to her,
comes alive when she calls it
by name. Nights when her life
is lost in other forests, fires here
go out, blankets are tossed by no one
to the floor. The dogs believe all night
the river is her car and rip the dark with howls.

I don't want to curse him with too much praise, but I think he is in the act of becoming one of the best romantic poets we've got. Which may not be as large a compliment as one suspects. How many yuppies, still worming their way along the neon floor of cancer gulch, are still romantic? Or is the compliment larger than one suspects? Perhaps. His metaphors dance and take you through turns you were not prepared for, and to your conservative consternation enjoy, because change, for once, is liberation:

In the darkness before dawn,
with the trees shaking their drenched leaves
above the roof in an erratic splatter
of sound, I move, transparent and ghostly,
through the house. Half asleep,
I am still thin with dreaming.
Light has not yet come to fill out this form,

to soak it pound by pound in the visible world,
to cover it with leaves of the real.

In boxing, there are subterranean dreams of being knocked down by blows so artfully delivered that they pound nothing out of you. The fall is free. You wake up refreshed. Breit can put three or four perceptions together in a row that have something like that effect. Some crusty old dead-ass sorrow in oneself is rejuvenated. Luke is a rainmaker. Put him in a desert, get him to recite, and clouds will gather.

In your bed, you feel
how death has plumped the pillow
and made the light bulb flutter
as if it was a candle.
You will not die tonight,
but it is closer than before.
And it is good to listen many times
to the world. It has sounds you can take
into the long silence.

If I could be a poet, I wouldn't mind at all being as good as Luke Breit.

— *Norman Mailer*
Brooklyn, NY
July, 1989

For Alice & Miranda

For Gratia & Harvey

For Yannis, Nicole & Kate

And For John, Cynthia & Patrick

*without whose love and support
this book would have been impossible.*

Table of Contents

from *In This Picture, We Are Laughing*

New Poems

About the author:

Luke Breit is the author of three earlier books of poetry: *Celebrating America Within; Words The Air Speaks;* and *In This Picture, We Are Laughing.* His work has appeared in numerous periodicals and anthologies. He is presently President of the Board of Directors of the Sacramento Poetry Center and for five years has been coeditor of *Poet News: Sacramento's Literary Review.* He is on the statewide Board of Directors of California-Poets-In-The-Schools.

Mr. Breit spent nine years as a top staff aide to the California State Legislature, most recently as chief-of-staff to one of its Democratic members. Since 1988, he has operated his own campaign and public relations firm, where he works on behalf of candidates committed to environmental and social justice issues. In his past, he has been a political reporter, newspaper editor, literary agent, publisher and editor, teacher, house-painter and bartender.

He lives in Sacramento, and is the father of two children: a son, Yannis, and a daughter, Nicole.

Celebrating America Within

San Francisco, California
1973

The Heart As Prisoner

for Miranda

Sentries stand in the dark corners
of the eyes. Behind them,
the prison camps fill with
the wounded soldiers from the inner world.
These words are the bullets that speed
through the walls of the mind
towards the eye. The guards fall.
You are so far away from me,
the prisoners must be
the tear that just now escaped
through the open fields of my face.

The First Day Home

I can't see it yet,
but I know it's just over those hills
in the distance:
dusk spreads through the tall grass.
Its huge fingers
close around the light.

Still, here, the light reigns
over burned grass
and sparse shrubs.
Out the window I see
the empty corral,
lonely and shimmering
in the last brilliance,
wanting a horse to kneel down
in its dark ground.

And I, I am alive
in my new home, desolate,
the country Wyeth dreamed.

All day, joy has been knocking
on this wooden door. All right.
I'm through suffering. Come in.
If you would stay, stay.
And be the wild galloping
in the dark ground of my heart.

Turning In

This afternoon I am concentrating
on the sounds between silences.
Above, the charred buzz of a fly
circles my head. To my right,
a loose piece of tin on the barn roof
is being strummed by fingers in the air.
Every now and then, an invisible plane
is rattling the windows of the sky.
And far off, an unknown machine
is churning air
into the solemn music of rust.

I have been too long
in the city, away from soil,
so my ears don't understand
this absence of sirens, the howls
of alley cats, the occasional scream.
This morning
I awoke before dawn
and shivered two hours
as dark silence prowled outside.

But I am beginning, again,
to listen to the silences
that rise up from fields
and rivers
and the roads
that are empty all night.

All Morning

All morning, I have been walking
through high grass, looking down
for snakes. In between the blades
of brown grass are the tiny prairies
and ranges of insects, their stillness
shattered by the great storms of my boots.
Liza, a dog
of no specific breed and fine companionship,
has been receiving mail
from the deep letter-boxes of soil.
Her nose begins to read
the soft cadences of earth
and, happy now,
she rolls in these pages of dust.
There are no snakes, but a butterfly
has just fluttered past my left shoulder
and vanished. I glance upward.
A light, milky blue begins to drift
across this canvas of sky.

Things Plunge

1

Finally, after thirty years, I rise
early enough to see the thick ropes
of a color no one has ever seen.
They swirl through the eastern sky,
plunge beneath the horizon,
invent the sun.

2

At noon, by the lake, things plunge:
a dog who thinks he is
a fish, a bird, the flash

I see in the corners of the world;
a boy dark in his secret imaginings;
me, on a rock, drowning
in the huge sea of a poem.

Listening To The Logs

1

In the afternoon, we enter
a clump of woods.
Most of the younger trees here
are dead, or dying;
their branches, like the thin arms
of the hungry, have strangled each other
for the precious drops of water.
The ancient ones stretch upwards
and survive, knowing that before
water drifts into the dusty mouths
of roots, it can fall
into the open hand of a leaf.

2

Underneath buzzing power lines
on the giant steel towers that sing,
when stroked, with the gleaming ecstasy
of machines, I realize I have not heard
the news for weeks. It's all right.
I point my human antenna
toward the clear channel of sky
to watch the beautiful reports
of weather.

3

In the chilly evening
we are listening

to logs turning in their bed
of fire. We age wine
in dark cellars of the mind.
In the drowsy heat, before sleep,
we dream of old
ornate movie palaces,
filled with gentle murmuring,
and the lights beginning to dim.

The Clear Coldness

We turn lights on
against fierce shadows;
burn thick chunks of forest
against the clear coldness;
wrap ourselves
in the thick insulation of gestures
against the sudden, strange burnings
in the other bodies.

Somewhere, a friend we do not know
is testing wings
that have sprouted
from his dark raging blood.
He tastes the salt in the wind,
steps into it,
soars above our lives
remembering the ancient dance.

Poem For Nicholas Ramirez

"Se amaran todos los hombres . . . "
Cesar Vallejo

In this small California town,
it is the beginning of winter.
The rain is falling
on the small stores,
on the post-office,
and on that bar
where I was so drunk and lonely.
It drips from the old redwoods
with the ancient color of freedom.
It is the color
Lorca and Hernandez saw in Spain,
and that Che saw in Cuba —
it made him drop everything
to climb up a rope
he found dangling in his heart,
flung down from the mountains.

Sweet Nick, dead now, saw the color
before any of us, in Spain
and Cuba too. I knew him well
during the years on North Beach,
his last revolution over
and the last poems written long ago.
I watched death fill up
that quiet life. Once, near the end,
he saw the color again,
looking into the young faces
that loved him so.

Posthumous Poem To My Father

I approach you half-drunk at midnight,
grandfather of my scattered children,
father to me, your orphaned son.
I didn't know if there was
a Heaven or a Hell, so, forgive me,
I've kept you imprisoned
in my heart these seven years.
Often I tried to set you free,
but you insisted on hanging onto
the sharp blade of a tear,
trying to slash your way out through my eyes,
and I had to shut you away again.

At home, I keep your poems,
stories, letters, in a bunch
of folders and envelopes.
They are all in an old milk-crate
I found one night in Chinatown.
I was drunk, and I thought
those Chinese symbols written on it
spelled your name. I still think so.
I don't let anyone live there
except us, so don't worry,
it's just been me these long years
you've felt there, in the darkness,
surrounding your life.

But all cages are insufferable
I guess, even these cages
of love. Tonight, I swear,
no matter what the pain,
I'm going to open it!
and that small moan my friend will hear
in the middle of this fierce night,
that will be you,
finally moving off into the air,
my love loosening into wings
to help you lift above the dark.

Beautiful Dreams

Once again, it is Tuesday,
the day each week when
I must return to the city.
Making sure the fire is out,
I pick up my bags, lock the door,
move down the muddy incline
to my car, and the long,
uneventful drive south . . .
but maybe today, for once,
something will happen:
a beautiful woman,
hitchhiking with her children,
will open her life to me
and I'll go in forever;
or a cop, in the rain,
will flag me to halt,
and I'll run him down,
disappear like a creek
into the earth.

Lines For Heavy Drinkers

In the evenings
when we are too wise
or too poor
to drink,
we wish to bless sleep
with our dry throats
and trembling hands;
so, we learn the same prayer
as the clerk of a small shop
in a bad neighborhood which,
like our eyes,
stays open all night.

Evening

Evening comes like this:

first it is just
those little trails of mist
you probably don't even notice,
there, just above the river.

Before long, it moves
up the beaches, hiding
in those long cold shadows
that you try to stay out of.

Suddenly, without warning,
it flashes like lightning
above the entire village.

When you come home
from the store
with your simple food,
you don't need to turn on lights
until you've taken off your coat,
and there's evening,
tumbling out of its sleeve.

You Are Sitting A Row In Front Of Me

for Richard Hugo

Last night, in bed, I read
one of your poems to my lady,
so we have come to this university
to hear you read. Two men
play with spotlights and other machinery,
believing they can capture your art
in their tiny cage of television.
The auditorium begins to fill up.

It is almost time. Suddenly, I realize
you are sitting a row in front of me,
somehow sprung up out of your book I carry,
a silent love blessed into shape.

Once, John Logan, a poet I love
as well, depressed, sought me out.
We got drunk and he spent
two days in my home,
drinking whatever was there,
searching my shelves for books he'd written.
One by one, he found them all,
and drawing ink from the drunk night sky,
signed each one for me.

Now, sober and dizzy in the harsh light,
you are before us.
Never mind the technology in the room.
You are autographing leaves of air
with signatures as pure as winds
that eagles love, and showing us the strange,
broken wings on which, somehow,
you have learned to fly.

Leaving the campus,
we return slowly
to our transient lives.
But as we enter the car, she,
who knew you less, perhaps,
than anyone there, said simply
"Thank you,"
wearing your scrawl on her heart.

Celebrating America Within

In Novato on Palm Sunday,
there is nowhere to eat
but at one of those chain restaurants
that yawn their dull breath at you
anywhere your car can get
fifteen towns to the gallon.
Outside the window by our table,
a few shrubs try to hide
the gray parking lot.
Little particles of death
fall forever on the main street beyond.
On her two hundredth birthday,
this is all America has come to;
even the great rumbling machines
can't cut more than an inch deep.
Past the Taco Bell, past McDonald's,
a freeway has cut a swath
through these living hills
and is gone
into the shuddering wilderness
of the north. Dark clouds
care nothing for our temporary towns.
They move between mountains
and the sea packed with the messages
of weather. They tell of how
Spring has been sighted
moving up from the south,
and of a rumor that his mother,
the earth, has reappeared,
shaking off her rags of winter.

Words The Air Speaks

Mendocino, California
1978

The Technology Of Forests

What comes from darkness holds the earth fast.
Roots deep beneath the ground
carry light to leaves, to bathe the air in green.
What's dark inside the heart is why we can't
see love until it's there,
is the path on which it comes.

This century stands finished in light.
From the air, cities gleam at you,
whatever the hour. Against our fear,
we plant our crop of streetlamps.
What's plastic and built for money:
a church's neon cross,
screws a thousand watts into the face.
Detectives in green rooms with one bare bulb
question the Catholic Mass
out of its robes of Latin
until it's a skeletal mass of holes,
the empty glare pouring through.

At night, at the bottom of any deserted road,
the earth steadies. Our eyes
focus to the dark again, the sky rounds
and becomes whole. Something in the air
shoots an arrow so straight the century
spins to gold, we begin to sing rivers
beyond their next bend, believing we can go on.
Deep inside are stored what we need to save,
these deep drifts of truth.

What Comes To Us

After dinner, after baseball
and beer, after heat, we walk
back of the old house, here
on top of the mountain, and shrink.
A thousand feet below,
between small lives
and our spinning globe,
a glacier of fog has thundered
silently in from the edge of space
and buried the world. The sun
floats gently down to this motionless sea,
and begins to drown.
It lends each wisp of cloud a color
to hurl at us, daring our eyes
to remember it. None do.
Instead, we retreat into caves of voice,
throwing them out loud and fast
as shelters against so much awe.
I move off, down the trail, to sit
alone and wait until the earth
has shrunk to a size
I can hold in my mind.
When it does, I'm by myself in night.
Suddenly lonely for my kind of animal,
I move back to the house
where the chatter, like evening,
has softened enough to be bearable;
I file what edges are left with wine.
Still, all night, our planet
is beautiful, still answers to "home."

Friday Night

Enough whiskey brings the strange bar
you're in up to you for introductions.
Slowly, any good saloon
finds how air shapes around you,
fills it the way a fine suit
begins to wear your life.
You're enough at home before too drunk
to buy a pretty girl a drink. That key
unlocks the night. You go in and find yourself
among old friends with familiar faces.
Their names hang on a ridge above your mind
waiting for a breeze
to float them down to tongue.

Across the street a dance rages
like an ocean of sound at high tide.
Dancers crest through the surface
of the bar you begin to trust,
then plunge back in again.
You hold the bar up and greet
each arriving contingent with whatever's right.
At two the night empties buckets into the dance.
Even that's tapering toward a quieter music.
People disappear the way
fog can suddenly break up, display a town.
Whatever warmth new friends mean
begins to find your cracks and drip out
until your voice is left with just one song,
the mournful one it's known too long.
A car opens to you; let it take you home.

In the morning, bed's empty
except for you. That other
was dream again. Your life's only child
is close but home's next door, the name
someone else's. You start again,
remembering that you're ten years older
than the age a dream you were having last night
kept splashing warm against your face.

What's Left

Last night, the old machine
under the coastal highway
churned fog out through every crack.
Drunk, with my friend Sally,
I fought that road forty miles
to home. My body kept making sleep
we didn't need. Sally knew.
She pumped me full
of any words that would
prop under my mind.
Somehow, we made it.
I dropped her off, headed in,
claimed the first familiar bed,
crawled into a cave of blankets,
rolled the rock of a pillow
into its opening.

In the morning, I check
the empty pockets anyway.
Coffee tastes bad but I drink it.
It's the kind of day I could lose friends,
but I'm alone in here. Outside,
a few pieces of sun struggle
down to the ground and are lost.
The river huddles close to its bed
and hurries past. A chain-saw
starts up somewhere among
the shy lives of trees,
begins to cut the way this Sunday
has left a gash in me. I try
to replant myself
in a deep soil of words.

Fourth Of July Parade In Point Arena

Sunday morning. In the spare church,
a few thin voices with organ try
to convince some distant god he's loved.
Outside, a battered parade stumbles by
like shipwrecked men beached up
beyond our town; shouts of our children
raise it past Easter parades in big cities.
This much we can do. Above,
a perfect sky teaches the other things:
that blue is a deep cave of silence
tilting away from us;
how a bird knows each drift of flight
is lifted to him like a prayer
from hands in the earth.
Wind floats us air so new
nothing's ever breathed it before;
our lungs bend into it like miners,
and come out rich. All things this morning
are cheap, but dear,
like buying up a mortgage on a life,
watching its ledger swing toward black.
We learn to measure music
by the lengths of simple towns
where small gods live, easy with children.

Some Days

Some days your life opens flat before you
like a desert, except it's teased by dreams of water.
You spend it searching for a hill to climb
but none grows. A break in the horizon
could mean cyclones to calm with a caress,
a word, some small piece of writing;
or the other: a fire you'd stoke
to burn open a door where passion might stumble.

Today a car comes down the road but turns around
and goes without a wave. For a moment
the children, small in the rear
keep looking back, wanting to see a river free,
to check a dog for the way a tail means friend;
the older ones up front see the house
is absent from the Triple-A Tourguide Map,
the lovely hanging foot-bridge not even
a thin line across the river,
and they hurry off. Even dust knows enough
to fill back the treads of tires
that meant some other road. The kind
that says "motel" when it should let go.

In the afternoon I finally let a decision bob me upriver
like a fish who has to spawn. I lie in the sun
and remember spawning with that pretty blond
last summer in the shrubs we'd gotten to
after dancing on hot coals of sand.
Lying on towels, knowing beneath sweat
the animal heat, had made it seem worth the try.
When I walk home now jagged rocks
are owned by shoe stores who think my sneakers
are too old, the wind's a different lust
against my back. Tonight maybe I'll have a drink,
cash a check and wait for her to float my way,
worry about food and rent some other wind.

Things To Believe In

Winter freezes the wood-stove switch
to "on" and leaves it there. On the porch,
the once huge pile of oak and fir
seem to shrink a full day's work each hour.
Still, as we move more and more to home,
our pile of friends keeps growing
and that teaches to warm with easy fires.

In this season, there are things
you must believe in: a car,
or some way to get you out; a fire
to wring you out when you're drenched in cold;
books whose words say "friend" in all
the languages a lonely day can speak;
a woman whose body becomes fire
when embers in the stove turn black.

Evenings she doesn't come are few, but empty.
The furniture of this house belongs to her,
comes alive when she calls it
by name. Nights when her life
is lost in other forests, fires here
go out, blankets are tossed by no one
to the floor. The dogs believe all night
the river is her car and rip the dark with howls.

Some nights when she sleeps
I go out for stars — not to count them,
but to be reminded of their ancient trust.
They give us our lives and bring
the nights to guide them, teach us
that the work of darkness is done by bodies
who build each other over and over
in the glow of distant suns.

It's easy to count the gifts we bring each other:
food and wine and quiet talk at home;
the smiles we use on each other as currency

during the business of the day;
a promise of a night out if money
that's supposed to happen ever did;
how our hands swim through darkness
toward each other
to keep the fragile lives they own afloat.

Getting Through

If light won't do it, a fire first thing
helps give the house to morning. Here,
in the woods, no morning paper's flung
against your door. You read the news
by currents in the air, how the fog lifts
or falls on the coast five miles off and down.
Specks of mist floating overhead
could be fires of friends you've never met,
but should. Find them, have them in to dinner,
and soon. They could be
that article you keep looking for
in magazines about how to fight what's lonely
and never find, and your pages might open
like buds, as if they were Spring.

But now it's still the morning. A car
going near is almost who
you've been hoping to see, but not quite.
The engine hums a tune, familiar, but off.
Last night you found her house empty
for the first time, came home and planned
your icy revenge. Now, it looks different.
If things had gone your way in that bar,
it might have been she approaching late
the house as empty as anything that's hollow,
she who'd imagine the foreign arms and thighs,
the laugh she wasn't meant to hear fading
just as she looked in. One of you
had to go first. This time, it wasn't you.

You relearn things. Cooking alone at night.
Straightening the bed mornings.
Cat food, laundry, shopping lists.
You adjust. Daylight shows you paths
to cross where she hasn't walked.
Nights, though, the house you live in widens
and a fragrance that you took for granted
still is in this air
that you thought came fresh each day.

Music Passing

for Rene

How the morning comes beautifully down
and opens the garden of your face;
how our bodies are the soft weight
drifting toward each other again;
how the drops glisten on your lips,
which have become my fountain;
how you perch above me,
knees by my shoulders, receive me
dry from the long night;
how the magic starts, again, again;
how the world has found a way
to teach us our names.

Your eyes are closed tight,
and I am loving
how sounds rush up wild
through whatever craggy trail of breath
is the way to find your mouth.
So close, your child watches us.
I imagine he is unbuilding us,
life-flake by life-flake,
finding his image in each crystal,
for he is where the world always points.
With a free hand I begin

to stroke his hair,
golden and lighter than wind
in this early light. He smiles
and a music starts,
moving through me like a storm,
like lava, reverberating sad and wonderful,
the music you hear
only once or twice in a lifetime
as it passes swiftly over the world.

I've tried to capture some of it
with words I spend hours
ripping loose
from this adhesive in my heart.
I offer them to you poorly,
the way a man long empty
suddenly thrusts a fortune
at someone he loves.
So here, take them, carved, as they are,
from your eyes, flashing in the dark;
from the boy lying calmly
in the dawn, his breathing
becoming the warm air around us,
from your voice, how it knew the way
to stroke whatever in me was empty
before this night swam toward us
like a thaw through a winter of ice.

To My Folsom Comrades

for Pancho Aguila

I awake at dawn. Down the ridge,
the ocean begins to flare.
Far back, behind mountains in the east,
the sun is striking this flint of day
against the earth; the morning catches,
and holds. Trees step out of the gloom,
become what they are again.
A chicken hawk circles above the cabin,
its cries over the earth
as lonely as a phone ringing,
over and over, through the night.

Tomorrow, I'll enter the gray stone
of my brothers' house: the prison.
They will be coming toward me
from cells I imagine
cold, damp and friendless.
To them each time I visit, I bring
what I can of the earth, and of gentleness,
concealed in these bags of poems.

To me they give, always,
the secrets of fire:
how to make a poem ignite
on the dead wood of a guard's eye;
how words can explode
like dazzling suns
in the ears of the deaf.

Human News

Dear Michele,

Sunday. Stayed up late again last night
for no important reason, except, I guess,
to avoid that empty space I lie alone in
most nights. The faces of friends are what I prop
between me and pain, even if the friends aren't close,
and the pain is nameless. Yours isn't.
Something beyond our lives
has been speaking to you
around every corner you've looked for months now,
shattering diamonds locked within you as if
they were so much cheap glass.
I read the letter of your brother's awful death,
put it away with the earlier one of your own illness,
the possible death you face,
and tried to forget they were there,
to go on about my life, to think that
what hurt in me was good enough
to get me drunk in bars
where I'd shut all sweet laughter out. Now,
on this pale Sunday, a hulk of newspaper
strewn worthless on the floor
because it has no human news,
I turn back to what you wrote.
I find the words where somehow your courage
still lets sparks of laughter in. They'll kindle
and I know you'll live. The voice that keeps
seeking you with horror will mellow
and turn friend. To me you said,
"Now I fight for my life with a rage,
for myself, by myself."
I say you fight for all of us,
bring us to the hard edge of a world deep enough
to know that when cold comes,
retreat is just the dance that keeps us warm.
Tiny seeds planted in you many springs ago
proved hardy,

have grown tall like pillars beneath a heart
I know pumps blood as rich as molten sun.
I go on with Sundays, with my life.
They're buoyed up somehow in this painful sea
because, like you, I've learned what I own is thin,
fits easily into one small life.

Love, Luke

Sunday Night

This night throws blackness over a sea already dark.
Waves splash against the sand, trail the way tears
leave streaks on skin. You learn wine
hangs as heavy on the heart
as the reasons why you drink it.
What you love's unsure, rustles like leaves scraping
all night against a yard filled with moonlight.
They fall, shadows between dark cuts
of the trees that let them go.
That's the way you try to let go
and can't. Friends you love want to know
what they have you need, to give it,
but they're asking after you've already
closed for the night. When you needed them
to share the slices you keep cutting out on paper,
they weren't hungry. They left you to feed strangers
who took the flavor, threw out the heart.

Now it's Sunday night and feels like it.
You know tomorrow can burst as clean
on the morning as first snow,
that what hurts sometimes slips
through ribs and hides behind your hills of blood.
Now, though, the pain is like clothing
you've worn uncomfortable
to a party where guests are all each other's friends.
In your skin they wonder why you're there,
where you shop.

Maybe you should be home alone,
a fire going hot enough
to burn what's ugly out of you. But this bar is lit,
the TV dulling as the wine and the wine cheap.
The chance you need of being recognized
by someone who knows that what you feel goes deep
is slim but there. Who knows?
That door could open any time,
she'd walk in still sweet enough
to gather you up, and haul you through her life.

Our Journeys

It is the gentle time
of late afternoon, when the day
begins its slow unbuilding.
A long garment of night
is being sewn in the distance
by the deft needle
of a song some unseen bird
has opened. Outside this window,
wind stirs like memory,
slightly lifts a veil of branches
to show the ancient face of trees.
Another day is gone
and we're all right, somehow.
The earth begins to soften.
A hawk trails by,
and night glides in behind,
its long arms
lighting the wicks of stars.

The Full Moon

The full moon
falls on the path,
my flashlight, for once,
not needed. Small buildings
in the distance
are stark in it,
as if the light
had drained them of life,
for the moon knocks
this hollow sound
against all of us.
One by one,
we shine back
our human answer,
these bare skeletons
blaze through the night.

In Baseball, It's The Bottom Of The Ninth

Today, the class I teach is slow,
my fault. I haven't found which lungs
breathe life into slight poems
whose source I know is deep.
Finding an excuse, I leave early.
Outside, a wind cuts through the yard
like a scalpel, piercing my dark clouds of skin.

Nearby, boys in sparkling baseball uniforms
poise their shadows, long in late sun.
They lean forward, high on toes,
ready to burst in whichever direction
a bat's explosion yells. Hand and glove
on knees, they'll wait nine innings
for a ball to veer toward them
the way a compass leaps to north.
No one watches them but me.

Beyond whatever lies or truths
are sprinkled on them like water,
now, on the field,
their blood is pure, racing clean
through the veins, hating no one,
knowing it owns only the years it wins
by losing ground to the one before.

Deep in right field, alone, I hurt.
My old glove sits on a shelf somewhere,
unused. Once in the bottom of the ninth,
I moved too easily under that round,
white third out,
ended a game and a way of life.
School stopped for me too that year.
The globe began to spin beneath my feet.
What I learned from then on
came hard but true,
I got back from the earth what I spilled into it,
no matter how the years slipped in between.
What's defensive in me always says
I'd shag fly balls nine innings
and never come up, to get back to what's simple.
Those days, on a baseball field green as morning,
I knew the grace of having that
which comes too easy, if it comes at all.

Closing The Eyes

Driving in the city,
the streets are old mine shafts.
Cars are chipped from their walls
and hurried out, thick as ore.
Light filters down between buildings
through a tent of haze,
piling up its fine dust all afternoon.

The city's mouth is against my ear.
It is opening and closing
on a small white pill of hysteria.

When I close my eyes,
the buildings drift into giant redwoods.
Light is sprinkling down
through green leaves
like cool water slipping between
the fingers of small stones.
And the road is a straight darkness,
leading to the silence an oven has
when it is filled with bread.

Finding Home

Late. On the hill home,
my feet sink into a soft dust
of privacy. Behind the blinds
where lights blink out,
lives are preparing to enter
each other.
The city softens with need.
I am almost to where I am going.
I have found my way
by the glow of this torch.
I scraped it carefully
from those corners of your face
where soft light lay hiding.

Rain

It's the second day of rain.
Green is running like blood
within the veins of grass.
Water rises in dark troughs of earth
and trembles through to roots
on the other side of air.
I would like to go with the rain
into this soil, so rich
with moisture, to learn
the silent roads that curve through trees
and the secret trails of flowers.
Now, the rain is planting
dawn into the ground. Soon, our hands
will harvest light from these fields.
Within the cocoon of each drop of rain
we can almost hear singing
as if something wild and alive
is about to burst free upon the land.

The Other Silence

Home at two. The silence
of these woods echoes its other silence.
A thick fog is the shield
between our brief lives
and the empty fairway of stars.
Even though my home's not cold
I build a fire for its comfort.
Outside, my dog finds
some void in the night
to plug with her barks.
And I sit before this paper
the faces of people I love
only now becoming
the words so soft
they spread like ash
upon this slash of whiteness.

Gathering The Morning

Up at dawn in the cold house
I put fire to graze
in the pasture of my stove.
Outside, the earth has slipped
into a soft gown of mist.
I step out
to gather up this air
like gold and store it
in the hidden cellar of my lungs.
Birds are singing
in the small church
of the woods,
and my dog, gone for hours,
steps out from under
these folds of mist,
the black harbor of her fur
glistening with night.

The Three Of Cups

for *The Folsom Prison Creative Writer's Workshop*

In fall, the earth brings forth
what we'll need
for the long months of winter.
Our simple gardens open
like a gift, our larders fill
as if they were gray clouds
beyond this crystal sky,
swelling with rain.
Our women lift cups of wine
from the grapes which have stained
these presses in our fingers. In the distance,
the work remains: roofs of our cabins
are still untarred, the firewood's still buried deep
within dead, gray trees.

Next week, this still air will fill
with the buzz of saws, churning our warmth.
For now, though, the earth
has thrust her joy at us.
We drink and eat
and lie beside our women
filled with this woven pleasure:
our lives, the world,
how they meet again
at the corner of each season.

On Visiting A Friend At The Hospital

When you leave, after good news,
and go for coffee in the early light,
your hands come together
above the steam
in the prayer
already answered.

Small Things

Here, tides of awe are not forecast
by weathermen on radio stations.
They come when they do, pledging each time
a measure of what's beautiful
shall be hummed into each life.
We stand on the earth, solid as wheat,
gentle as roots, targets for anything
that the world aims, and cocks.

A Time Of Coldness

for The Natural Food Store Collective, Point Arena

In a time of coldness
a planet can wither
like last ears of corn, alone
in an open field of wind.
Streams and creeks dry up
while wells of the rich
rot useless as money
in dusty vaults.
Some men have pockets
that lock tight as jaws,
wear smiles brittle as ice.
They stuff cotton in their ears
and live in tall graceless buildings
that creak and sway
above the cries of the poor.

Some of us come together, out of need.
At times, we trip
over small stone walls of our pasts,
and use them to build new houses. We find
that together we're stronger than money.
We learn how a town can be a world
and, by sustaining it, we prop a pillar
under the corner of everything that sags.
The tiny fire we've lit, of friendship,
of working together, warms us well,
and its flames lick high
and glitter
on the stone fortresses of the mighty.

Wages

Inside, there is a darkness singing
of an ocean the full moon carries
in its sack of light.
We haul the weight of one wave
across the continent of night.
This is the job the moon pays us for
in grains of sand:
footprints we leave for the hands
of each new tide
to carry up from the earth,
messages
left for the sea,
this gift,
our human salary.

Brushing Against Stars

Beyond the headlands,
moonlight is skating
across the water.
Between the crashing
of the waves,
a great silence
is lifted up to us
by the hands of night.
It is an emptiness
that has traveled through space
unravelling its threads of sound.
Even talking quietly,
our voices scrape against it;
they too have traveled
the great journeys of our lives,
gathering the dust of stars.

Shelter

for Sharon Doubiago

It's one a.m. Good fire resounding through my stove
like music, like Christmas carols,
how, when they're sung well,
they fill up the quiet streets like snow. I wonder what
Christmas was like in L.A. You couldn't seriously
have been waiting for snow
the way we always did in New York.
Now we're locked together in this small northern town
where we know Christmas
offers neither snow nor warmth,
just this strange in between that we've learned to believe
is weather. Well, it gives me something to believe in.
Your two children have grown firm and strong without
a Macy's Santa Claus to tickle childhood dreams. Once,
a child, I asked that phony old Saint Nick,
whiskey on his breath,
for peace on earth. Now, twenty-five years later,
I ask it still. Outside the house, the woods creep up
to the window, like they always do. Trees stamp and toss
outside, scattering this morning's rain
in gusts against the roof.
Here, peace seems that easy: something you could fill
cupped hands with, like water,
and share with whoever's thirsty,
and Sharon, everyone is. I watch football
on TV and think of how your son could grow into that,
like James Wright said, "galloping terribly against
each other's body." The world's cold
and all these human fires
we light, of poems, of sharing, is all the warmth there is.
Don't blame me if I guard it all so jealously —
it's not hard to believe the world is Alaska
and these poems are coats. Wear them gently
and never sell them no matter how warm it seems.
I know what we do is good: one ear listening
is a cabin thrust up hot around us. And know,

in this Christmas season, that I love you.
I love all of us who believe that language is the knife
that spreads what we feel
onto the dry crust of someone's heart.
I hope we spend some time. I like it
when I feel your life as true around me as the inside
of flame. Wherever you go, don't go away.
Let all our days be as holy as Christmas
and Christmas a time when all the gifts we offer
are the true ones of the heart, simple gifts
of some door continually opening that can't be shut.

It's done. You are fine enough to shelter all you love
and big enough to love more than you can shelter.
If that's a contradiction, forgive me.
I'm no logician, only a poet. I give what I can
from whatever shelves inside me are still laden.
Sometimes it's enough. Like now. Keep warm.
Your friendship is the hot spiced wine
I keep dipping my cup in. Merry Christmas.
And a New Year filled with simple resolutions
we've always kept: paper filled with poems
good enough to keep trees from weeping.

Mendocino

Some days the afternoon
holds the day tight in its brilliant palm.
The sun pauses above the horizon
for hours which grow huge and round,
hollowing out this rim of gold.
Walking out on the headlands,
I see the ocean's ancient
carving of the land continue.
Here, where America ends
and becomes the sea again,
a rich crop has been planted
firmly into the soil.

A quiet peace has been established,
for the land knows it must give way
to water and salt, and the residents
are simply tenants of the earth once more,
filling up with the simple wisdom
the world is always teaching.
Now, even the afternoon must give way.
The pale sky begins to bloat with color.
And above,
the buds of stars are about to burst.

Cantata

Trails from the woods
meet behind this house.
On them, after darkness,
after the lights from surrounding homes
fade like radio stations in the midwest,
the ancient inhabitants
of this small forest begin to stir.
Now, the true music of the earth,
packed with silence, begins:
a deer forages in the brush
for her simple meal;
frogs court each other
in tongues that rasp over
the sandpaper of love;
a cricket finds the note the wind sings
and measures it
with the yardstick of his voice;
and I,
burrowed in this wooden cave,
am part of it too,
making my own human music
of listening
and transcribing.

A Winter Solstice Poem

for Jay & Monique Frankston

Looking at the newspaper headline
that my friends have taped above my desk:
"Poets, despair not!" I feel the earth
moving dark beneath my feet.
Out in the stillness
a lone truck grinds its gears and fades by.
The dogs roll in the damp night grass,
sniff each other, their tails beating
the strange rhythms of the ancient world
that they cannot know, but do.
Above the heavy clouds that have
hung over us solemnly for days,
the stars are as bright as ever,
and somewhere within them,
living beings ponder, I'm sure,
all the things we do.
Life stretches back
into the roots of the universe
and bursts into flower on one
of the infinite globes every moment,
for the hand of god is the hand of a farmer
who cannot resist the touch of soil,
even though he knows what he plants must die.
We are this wheat he harvests
each autumn the universe turns.
I do not despair, I am singing,
remembering I am a part
of this bread of god.

What The Earth Writes

for Dawn

Tonight, on the road,
a young doe and her fawn
are such beautiful gravity
my car is dragged to a stop.
I sit, stilled and joyful,
watching these graceful prayers
the earth has uttered.
For a moment we are thus,
a confrontation between the black wilderness
and the icy spotlights of civilization,
until the world,
like an elastic band,
snaps her creatures
back into her story,
the one that never ends.
And I, alone again with my machine,
plunge forward through the night toward this page
and the words
I will try to fill with awe.

Birds

They are the words
that the air speaks.
Perched on the lips
of the wind,
they drift off
into meaning.
Some afternoons,
the fields grow dark
with their graceful language.

In This Picture, We Are Laughing

Sacramento, California
1987

Letter To Dawn

Dear Dawn,

It's morning again. From here I can't see
what your window echoes, that vast expanse that makes
us understand how much each day can shake the world.
It shakes me to think that I may never
wake to that world again, never again
be caressed by the way you feel it, by that
vision of yours that excuses all pain and makes
all our life together once again so infinitely worth it.
In my eye I sometimes see
your daughter come slowly up the stairs
as the first light begins to pry up the edge of darkness,
how you slide over to make room for her,
how the flair of your back presses against my flesh,
your hair carelessly drapes across my face . . .
Oh I know I loved you too much
and so do not love you enough,
but it's only my failing to understand why wheat grows,
why the sky lifts us away from the grave, why I go on
loving you against the weight of the universe
pressing down on my heart with its icy fingers.
What I do understand
is how to get up in the morning, how to order coffee,
how to believe the morning paper tells things
it's important to know.
Sometimes though, glancing back, I see you
getting the cereal out for your daughter,
see you moving around on the bare wooden floor,
and how beyond you the world spreads out,
the sun lifts above the mountains,
all before this window, this thin sheet of glass
that is like some mirror that never lies.
Love, Luke

Alone In My House

In the darkness before dawn,
with the trees shaking their drenched leaves
above the roof in an erratic splatter
of sound, I move, transparent and ghostly,
through the house. Half asleep,
I am still thin with dreaming.
Light has not yet come to fill out this form,
to soak it pound by pound in the visible world,
to cover it with the leaves of the real.

Now, there is light through the trees.
Far off, a rooster begins his preening cry.
Darkness is rising up from the steaming ground,
gathering itself up from the floor
of the battered tool shed, to softly graze
the lips of each leaf
as it moves off toward the west.

Nearby, a car begins. On the slick roads,
others begin to roll. In the restaurants,
waitresses sip the last of their coffee,
set the last table. Eggs are poised,
bread hovers over toasters. Letters
from friends are rushing towards us.
Alone in my house, I speak aloud,
and the day catches and ignites.

The Key

Before light, you awake in the damp bag.
Sitting up, you see the dark mass of the ocean,
hear its hollow pounding upon the earth's door.
Getting up to pee, you feel the cold sand
squeezing between your bare toes.
Above you, the cliffs loom like great birds,
trying to push off into the air.
Further, you know, are the houses.
People are sleeping, families.
Maybe one of them used to be yours
in some way you don't understand anymore.
Maybe the key you always find in your pocket
fits some house, some sleek new car,
some office, maybe even someone's heart.
Now it fits only
the lock of sand you force it into.
It turns and the earth's door opens to you.
You are going to step into it now.
Behind you, the first light begins
to knock down the flat, cardboard houses.
No one is screaming.
No one is calling your name.

A Summer Evening

In the dark, late, my mother
sits on the porch with a last cigarette.
It is Maine, and though she cannot hear
the sea, she is sure that she smells it.
She does hear the moths
slapping against the wrought-glass shade
on the porch light, and something else
she thinks might be
the rustling sounds of her cat,
out hunting in the fine darkness.
She is not grieving, but there is

an almost sweet sadness
surrounding her like white gauze
as she thinks back
over the long stretch of years.
There is something about meaning
she is trying to remember,
some truth she thinks she learned
long ago, but it is as elusive
as the last snatch of a dream,
caught just upon waking,
the rest, going, gone.

She does not fear death,
but she is surprised to find how little
she understands it; she'd supposed
as she moved down the long line of years,
its clear and definite outline
would have swum out of the mist toward her
and filled her with its promise.

Now she looks up at her beautiful gray home
built by her friend, a boatyard's master carpenter,
to house her, my sister and I. She'd thought
to make a place for all of us,
a good home, strong and a little ancestral,
for the continuation of the lineage.
But none of us are there.

In the woods, the cat is silent,
watching her. He is entranced
by the incredible arc the bright red tip
of her cigarette makes as she brings it
to her lips and how it glows even brighter
in the absolute darkness of Maine.
She stands and calls him to come in,
this other small member of her family,
there at least. All night he will lie
by her feet on the clean blanket, breathing quietly,
listening to her breathe, alive,
alive, and filled with meaning.

Writings On The Heart

In the sheriff's office,
the fat cop separated us.
Me he shoved in the broken cell,
the bed so crippled
it rocked up and down all night
like a formica table in a cheap restaurant,
the toilet seatless and encrusted,
the walls encrusted with the familiar words:
"28 days to freedom and pussy";
"Barney sucks cock";
"Fuck niggers and spics."

We were just 65 miles from Mexico,
the wetback we'd picked up
hitching in Houston, my friend, and me.
The car dead and junked for twenty dollars,
we flagged the one wrong car
and ended up watching high school girls
through the bars twice a day,
five days a week, for a month.

I was sixteen, pretending to be unafraid.
No phone call, no charges filed, no judge.
The FBI came in the middle of one night
and dragged off the wetback, our friend,
whose address was written on my arm
because they wouldn't give us paper.
For once I wished my father powerful,
a battery of lawyers arriving from New York,
the hick sheriff gulping nervously as he turned the key,
asking for our forgiveness. Instead,
one pretty high school girl brought us cheeseburgers,
and asked me to come and see her when I got out.

Yes, I had dreams in the flat, hard night
of being hung,
of lynch parties yelling for my blood
for drinking bourbon in their sacred town,

for dreaming lonely of that high school girl
who brought me food, for traveling with
a Mexican who had taken some white man's job.

Instead, thirty days
and a fine that took almost all we had
levied by a judge old enough to be his own father,
and then finally the ride with the young men who
screamed 90 mph down that straight rode to Mexico
where they would get drunk and laid that night.
In the late afternoon, I looked back
through the rising dust at that town: Freer, Texas.
It lay there, unchanged by my thirty day visit
except, maybe, for a book of poems
I'd left with a high school girl.

We didn't cross the border with
those reckless Texans that night,
but put in at a motel in Laredo.
We were tired, and we thought it wise
to prop at least one night
between that new land
and Texas.

The Question

"What is the meaning of life?"
he asked over and over again.
He staggered above me in the full moon,
thin, handsome, arrogant, drunk.
We were fifteen,
on the beach near my father's summer house.
Our sleeping bags lay open on the sand
and in the distance
we could hear the dark ocean swirl and foam.

More than twenty years later,
the rain rages on a house

three thousand miles away.
I call it home.
Nearby, another ocean
works tirelessly,
resculpting the ageless cliffs.
And even now, sitting with coffee
at my desk, something of a success
in my own life, I remember
the challenge I felt, and finally
the embarrassment at not knowing the answer
to your silly schoolboy question:
"What is the meaning of life?"

And all the while
waves on the sand,
answering.

Friends

for Dawn

In the morning, we are standing, somehow
still together, looking out to the sea.
"I saw the great leap of a whale," you tell me,
and I think how the earth always stops for you,
holds its picture firm and steady as if
you were some great friend.
Where you touch soil food grows, or flowers.
Plants you call by name stay your friend,
even in the dark time. And I,
having gazed long at the ocean
to hold just one whale in my real eyes,
still wait for god to aim one at me.
And I, finally putting my arm around you again,
feel how the god I do not know, but almost believe,
holds you so carefully in his calloused palm.

Finding You

This is how it comes.
A bottle drops and breaks
and night seeps out.
One by one, stars rise
to the surface
of the heavy liquid
and swirl into focus.
Now, the bulls in the far pasture
must begin their long dream
of afternoon.
It seems I can predict it,
all of it:
how I will sip wine
and tend the fire, and then
finally think of you.
You are reading in bed,
your eyes growing heavy.
You are dreaming of me
inside your body,
snuffing out the faint candles
down each corridor of bone.

Moving In

Tired and sweaty, you come to a stream.
The sun is dappled through
the great shadows of the redwoods
skimming like little gold specks
over the water. It is cool here.
You undress and with cupped hands
begin to lift the water toward you
like a prayer. In the clear stream
you can see how ragged your beard has become,
how disheveled your hair.
Finally clean, you turn to your
mud-caked clothes, stiff with perspiration.

You have nowhere to go.
Behind you, in a clearing,
is a small cabin, deserted.
You know whoever lived there
is not coming back. You do not remember
your name or where you have come from.
Small animals watch your progress.
Birds are singing high in the branches.
For all you know,
you have never even seen a city.
You won't have to make any decisions
until the weather comes.

The Singing

Above the trees, the full moon
holds us at beam's length.
We strain against the pale leash of light
to break free, to hurtle through space
as alone and wild as we were
when the gods were drunk and reckless
and we were truly made in their image.

God is stark now, pious with paper-thin hands
transparent in the pale moonlight. We pray to him
at set times, no more by the emptying of wine skins.
We have become gray-suited, our short hair
a sign of determination, of our important goals.
Still, some evenings, one of us
breaks loose and leaps into the sky.
The rest of us become still.
Inside our bodies,
we feel our old fur ruffle.
Memories of tribes, campfires,
animals damp with night,
begin to stir. And above,
almost too dim to hear,
the ancient, joyous music still sounds.

The Snake In Your Eyes

for Meca Wawona

Down below, in the cities,
people are just now entering
the long cave of evening.
Here, on the mountain, it is already late.
Your daughter sleeps silently
in the loft above, and you
are bent over the last figures and words
of the work you do
to heal the earth.

Across the room from you I sit,
half in your world, half in mine.
I do not know about the rattlesnake
approaching the door, how we will stand
in fright and awe, seeking a way
to protect ourselves
yet save the beautifully uncoiling snake,
and find it. I just know that you
have uncoiled the long braid
of your hair and in the soft candlelight
it is undulating like water
down the long fall of your back.

Suddenly, the loud rattle. Without speaking,
we are together at the door.
The small snake moves ominously
in the dust, singing
its beautiful warning. I watch you
watching the snake. Your eyes
fill to the brim with the full moon.
A few feet away,
love is dancing on the earth.

Getting Ready

At dusk a bird begins
so clear it could be
the signal for some
gentle attack upon your cabin.
Beyond the thin forest
the Indians are beginning to gather,
silently dismounting
the damp horses. You sit
at your desk, sipping coffee.
A stream of smoke
lifts from your chimney
like a finger stirring
in the inverted cup of the sky.
Now you hear the clear birdcalls
loud.
The Indians are walking softly
on the trail towards your house.
In a moment you will see them.
You are alone, whistling, washing cups.

Making Up Stories

We came into town slow that day.
Small erratic breezes lifted dust,
then settled it before our eyes.
We stopped in the filling station
to get the car put back right.
Then, last supplies for the long trip.
Finally, the saloon, just the one
on the seaward side of the sleepy street
I remember, for the couple of beers
that always remind you you're traveling.
The barmaid was cute,
flashing shy, come-on smiles. I liked her,
so I made up a story, not better
than the real one,

but one she'd remember more easily:
less complicated,
fewer relationships ending badly,
less silly drunken binges,
less about how poetry was the journey
I had taken into darkness.
We stayed longer at that saloon
than we intended. When we left,
the neon was already buzzing in the dark
above the bar. In the car,
I let my friend drive. As we followed
the street lamps out into the looming night,
I wondered if there is only one empty spot
each stranger you will never see again
fills in you, or rather if there's enough of them
to go around all the strangers you'll ever meet
and love for a moment,
enough of those empty spots maybe
to go around all of them twice.

An American Poem

Further up the road you have been
walking all day you see the town.
One tall steeple of the white church
tells you its name, who owns it,
how people look at each other
over the high hedges. Film still takes
ten days to develop at the drug store
and high school girls stay virgin,
willing to wait for the long,
slow grinding to begin. Dogs bark
all night here, but are friendly,
and the Veterans of Foreign Wars
have nobody to contend with
but the one high school English teacher,
a conscientious objector, a small hero
to a few of the sensitive ones each year.

Five years ago, you'd have stopped here
in this small town, where you could almost believe
America was innocent and blameless again.
The fields around the town, though,
are soaked through with the same chemicals,
and just now the Wonder Bread truck passes you,
the dust drifting up in the slow air.
Fifty miles on is the city, the lights
and glitter, the tapestry of women who will hold you,
the drinks in the all-night saloons,
the way life and death slug it out each hour
every block. You hitch your pack up high
on your shoulders and set off,
not even a look back at the town even now
softening with evening. The years are back there.
Your future is ahead, where America
rounds the curve past innocence forever,
and the hot nights wait to burn their scar
deep across the shattered mirror of your heart.

Sacramento

The movement of air northward
flutters and turns the pages of the seasons.
In another time, I would by now
be preparing for winter. At dusk,
when the heat of the day
had begun to seep into the ground,
I would be splitting the great logs
of oak and madrone, redwood and cedar,
piling them peacefully one atop the other,
the brilliant flame hidden in the heart of each.
Mornings, I would check the roof
for obvious leaks, the walls for wind tunnels,
the stove chimney for clogs
that could force fire from its seams
out to join the passionate wood walls.
The store of good books would already be

settling in under the eaves
of the coming, private time.

Here, the change is barely noticeable.
A slight drop in temperature,
the breeze cooling off the evening,
jackets in the darkening streets.
But there is no sense of urgency,
of important tasks undone
and the weather about to unbuckle the world.
Here, there are thermostats
that will lock winter outside
to swirl and howl aimlessly about.
The worst winter storm
will not even make the lights flicker
nor interrupt the glaze of the new television season.
Instead of the homes of friends and neighbors,
there are the bars, the restaurants,
where we sit so close to each other
our sleeves kiss in moments
when the waiter's back is turned.

Here, in winter, our houses ride it out
without the need for our participation.
Temperatures target themselves
towards our maximum comfort.
When things go wrong,
there are telephone numbers to call,
experts to make repairs.
The only unexpected knocks on the door
are the ones to fear.
No one has been out in the cold
picking berries all day,
standing outside your door in the frosty air,
both her breath and the warm pie she carries
steaming in the pale moonlit night.

Looking Back, What Eyes Fill With

The town was half closed down when I pulled in.
The only bar was thick with lives
tangled and indistinguishable from the drinks
the barman with the tattooed arm
believed the air would pour.
Down the street, the movie theater,
all lights out and letters missing
from the next film's title,
held steady two days above Friday night
when the town would sweep into it like a wave.

Nearby, the liquor store and deli
shipped boxes of Oly, Coors and Bud
onto the waiting backs of pickup trucks
growling at the curb. A few streetlights,
a few more stores, some houses,
an old condemned building kneeling into the earth,
the deputy gliding silently by, over and over,
like an echo the county seat
had crooned into the night,
and the knowledge, somehow,
that a mile down the road
was the sea.

Not a bad town, mostly quiet,
its dreams dusty with summer
or drenched in the long dark season,
not quaint enough to attract the hordes.
But through the cracked white paint,
the unrepaired sidewalks,
the words on roadside advertisements
fading in the fog like so many old memories,
the charm of that town rose
on the wings of the gulls that had owned it
before the first Russian choked hard
at the sight of a Redwood,
even before the old Pomos, eyes red with weeping,
crossed the mountains and discovered

the holy food of the sea,
those gulls who still carry the town aloft
into the air pierced with their haunted cries.

Just beyond, the river stretches indolently
down from the small coastal range.
Salmon and steelhead spawn there.
I stopped and listened hard for a couple of years
in a small cabin by the river. I made a friend or two,
wrote and fished and swam and dreamed,
then drifted on.

I still walk down that mainstreet now,
anytime I climb through the
the good window of the past.
There, just beyond the bend, a river
joins the sea in understanding,
and the old, unpainted houses
shake off the early morning fog
and stand dazzling
in the clear, sun-splashed, ocean air.

Why We Listen

Some nights, a moment arrives.
The firm ground starts to slip away from you
and death nods beautifully at your side.
Now it is time to listen to the world again,
to hear how water is sucked into roots,
how thin wings lift on the sheets of wind:
each time, it may be the last time.
In your bed, you feel
how death has plumped the pillow
and made the light bulb flutter
as if it was a candle.
You will not die tonight, but it is closer than before.
And it is good to listen many times to the world.
It has sounds you can take
into the long silence.

Small Charities

Early on a Saturday morning,
a light drizzle coating the windows
with privacy, the swarthy, silent man
who lives across the street
is raking leaves into a big pile.
The leaves are damp and their dank,
sweet odor lifts itself like brewing coffee
to his nostrils. He is no longer young,
but some days he works around the yard
of the old woman down the street,
tidying up, getting the leaves
into the gutter for the truck
which bursts some mornings into
the neighborhood's collective dream.
Other days, he visits the elderly gentleman,
stricken by stroke, and talks softly to him
as they walk slowly down the street.
He is helping as he can.

He does not think of himself
as particularly generous, the swarthy man
who lives across the street, whose name
I do not know but who has quietly
introduced himself to me many times
over leaves and neighbors' fences.

There are men in faraway places without neighborhoods.
They speak of charity and the goodness
of helping those with less,
then casually turn to aim a bomb.
They do not know of the large,
gentle man across the street,
of his unsung deeds, and if they did
they would not understand, or care.
Yet they stir uneasily in sleep
as his long shadow falls silently
across their brilliant fields of death.

Softly Hunting

Together, but separated by the bar,
we are trying to unbuild a distance.
You are moving very well, a hunter,
through this forest of bottles.
Maybe the piano music is the wind
playing in your hair as you stalk
each customer, maybe your bullets
are lighting fires down the corridors of dry throats —
but I am moving well too.
When you finally look at me
you see that you are lined up in the sights of my eyes.
We stand there, two gentle hunters,
aiming the loaded questions at each other.
Outside, the cold winter pauses on a ridge.
We have just
the one warm pelt between us.

Visiting That Country Again

Near the log where we sit, my son
hovers dangerously, I imagine,
near the cliff's edge: beyond,
a steep slope and then, too quick,
the sea. I call him nervously
to stay close. Next to each other
for the first time in our lives,
you are smiling.
I wonder if you know how your hair
has been flirting with the sun again.

All afternoon, you have told me your story
in the language of listening. Have you taken
my words into the cool darkness
at the backs of your hands? Turn them slowly over
and you will see
they are tiny, golden butterflies

bringing you only those few gifts
thin, trembling wings are able to bear.

We get up, the boy on my hip. Below,
I think the sea must change somehow
when people near her are changing.
You think so too, I know.
On the path,
the soft music of your hand
drifts into mine.

Richard Hugo: In Memoriam

You wrote gold.
You said things that struck chords
no composer dreams.
You never said you'd had enough of life,
but you felt things too deeply
to stay alive,
even as briefly as you did.

You loved James Wright,
he died. You loved Muriel Rukeyser,
she died.
Neruda died too,
and Vallejo of starvation
raising money for the Spanish loyalists
to fight the General Franco
who shot Lorca
and let Miguel Hernandez
die of pneumonia in a dungeon cell.
Others cut off Victor Jara's hands
to prevent him from leading
the doomed Chileans in the soccer stadium
in the songs of their land.
He led them anyway, with stumps
you remember, so they opened up with their guns.
That stopped him.

Some of us who are still here, Richard,
might not be if not for you.
You sang our loneliness eloquent,
you counted our losses human and dignified.
Sometimes in bars, I'm pleased to find
your book in my pocket
like running into an old friend.
I share my drinks with you and think
how you could write better
with both hands tied behind your back
than just about anyone on the planet,
and how that's almost exactly the way you did it.

Now maybe it's only a time to miss you,
like we miss James, and Muriel. But understand,
it's all we can do, for we don't know who
they'll come for tomorrow, except
it will be one of us. It always is.
We die easily because
we're the only ones who die
when the words aren't true.

But Richard, I have a son.
And he's going to know you,
I promise. When he is rebuffed,
first time, by a girl, I'll read him
about why you think of Dumar sadly,
how you walk home from the dance alone,
wondering what it is you do wrong.
And when it is time for him to vote,
I'll show him your book,
What Thou Lovest Well, Remains American,
so that he can know
how deep things occasionally go in this land.
And when I die,
I pray it will be your words that he'll read aloud,
drunk and angry, in some great old bar
that men build for these occasions.

Where You Go

for Yannis at age five

That beautiful boy with the golden hair
that curls notoriously
around the intense, almost ancient eyes,
is finally asleep in his soft room.
I do not know what great good thing I have done
that the world should have made me so fine a gift,
only that I know now for sure we are here,
this final, only son — his final, only father.

"What you doing, dad?" he asks, although
I have told him the answer several times.
He has not yet learned his elders' belief
that the answer is always the same;
for him, anything straight can swerve.
And does.

Why not?
An hour into his sleep, I go into the room
and see, by dim nightlight, his familiar form
curled beneath the covers.
But I cannot stroke his hair,
nor graze his cheeks with my lips,
he is gone so deep now into the darkness,
that place beyond sleep into which only small children
and the very old sometimes suddenly slip.

As for me, I'm plucked too far from one
and drawn too quickly toward the other,
and I tremble to see him so lost to that other world.
I type, I type, to know I'll be here when he returns,
the gentle tapping of the keys
my only anchor to the earth.

Why I Love To Run Early

Very early, I go out to run.
It is still cold, and the fog
has closed down the city with silence.
A woman, waiting for the bus,
starts as I loom up out of the mist.
Besides her, no one yet.

In the park, I am alone with grass
and trees, with empty tennis courts
and a library whose books
are still and wordless with sleep.

Now, a few cars
and a solitary man, already out
walking his dog, a blurry red
Irish Setter streaking through the park.
Now I know why I love to run early,
before the traffic starts,
before the world awakes.

It is because
those few of us out so early
are still as soft
and shimmering
as dreams.
If we pinched one another,
we could find ourselves curled in our beds.
But we do not touch, do not speak,
we move almost transparently,
as ghostly as anything
this world of the living
has ever breathed.

Tents At Livermore

for Cole Swensen

Dear Cole,

I've been wandering listlessly around
the Cotati compound where Michael lives all day,
waiting for you to arrive, watching the young people
sunning their lithe vessels near the water. Musically,
you'd approve of the day: Bob Marley,
the cynical infusions of Randy Newman,
and I plan serious injections
of Duke Ellington later in the afternoon.
Maybe part of this listless feeling
is that we went to see *The Grapes Of Wrath* last night,
Henry Fonda perhaps the screen's first great anti-hero,
the black and white photography etching Steinbeck's
simple but true message of justice
deep where we carve such things.
All day I've been thinking
of the protestors in the tent jails
at the Livermore Weapons Testing Lab, wondering why
I'm not there, wondering why
I've stopped putting my body
where my heart so clearly is.
Maybe I'm just forty and comfortable,
not sure what works politically any more. Still,
there they are, the papers and TV say,
singing and praying
for an end to the nuclear madness. Have you noticed
how local six o'clock Eyewitness News reporters
love to film people saying, "These weapons
are what protect their right to protest!"
In a dream the other night, Cole, I saw
thin, long silvery missiles
float slowly across the sky.
I haven't had a dream like that since 1961
and the Cuban missile crisis,
Kruschev's and Kennedy's boats

and missiles poised at each other as if the ocean
were some large bathtub. Kennedy, a Catholic,
prayed each night and finally knew he'd been wrong.
These new men aren't like that.
They know they're the end
of that particular lineage. They'd rather
take us all out in one big blast
than give the world to women, children and poets.

Well, Michael will be home from brunch soon,
we'll put on Rolling Stones records or watch the game,
make wine coolers and sit by the pool, hoping
for serious bikinis. The sun will pick its precarious way
through the clutter of satellites
to the horizon. Somehow, the world, however damaged,
still goes on. The people in the tent jails
eat county-supplied meals and plan their strategy
to save the world.
The rest of us find whatever strength we need
to go on with out lives,
holding on to the one anchor of sanity,
in tents at Livermore.

Who Will Remember?

for Ace High

Driving up G Street to home,
the light rain is singing,
"You'll turn 40 this year,
alone."
Mornings, still drenched in sleep,
I prowl my few rooms,
searching for wives, children,
even dogs or cats, some small sign
of domestication, someone or something
to remember I'd been here today
if I passed on tomorrow.

Out there in the world, in the rain,
there are by all accounts some two thousand people,
many of whom I have never met,
who have possessed at least for a time
one of the books that I have written,
books that turn up in the used book stores
gratifyingly only now and then.
Others are in obscure corners
of the bookshelves of old friends,
remembered mostly when I send cards saying,
"Remember my book?
The one you said you liked so much?"

One friend always has it on his bedside table
even when I show up unexpectedly.
If he wants a drink, I buy it for him, you bet.
It's not a wife, not my son living with me,
but it's something, by god,
something he's heard from me that's strong
or true enough
that he keeps my book there by his bed,
something solid there for him
when his own wifeless and childless life
is tossing and turning on the wide sea of night.

Letter To Sean From San Diego

> *One man loved the pilgrim soul in you,*
> *and loved the sorrows of your changing face.*
> —William Butler Yeats

Dear Sean,

Here is the letter I always promised I'd send —
years late and from a place so soft and lonely
I think you would cry.
Of course you would. Sean, you cannot take a walk

around the block here without seeing one of the most
breathtaking girls you've ever seen,
on the weekends three or four at a time.
They wear almost nothing and for the first time
you understand the expression,
"There ought to be a law." There really should.
We men could die of confusion if we listened to those
who tell us what we feel is just lust,
when we know for sure
we've fallen deeply and forever in love
at least eight times today. Already.
I don't know just what it is men do die of:
bullets in wars, occasional fancy fiery jet crashes —
Sean, I think I can remember
when men could die of sadness.
I don't want to die, but I want to go back that deep.
I want to know what women think
when they stretch those tiny strips of cloth
over lovely breasts,
all the soft globes and valleys of flesh.
It's easy to sit here in a motel
with the ocean fifty feet away,
and feel superior: "I'm a poet, by god!
I've fought and won important battles while these kids
were in diapers," I think, fuzzy with wine,
wondering why that blond with no clothes on to speak of
is holding hands with that gorgeous surfer kid
instead of being up here, listening to these sad poems.
When it comes right down to it,
he's surely a lot more fun
than me, young and lusty enough to fuck all night
without once envisioning his own death.
Hell, if I were her I'd be with him too.
Sean, there's nothing like a motel on the beach
to put you in touch with your maker.
Cut off from everything easy and familiar,
you stroll out to the water's edge
and stand amazed at stars and that thin sliver of moon,
to see so clearly how filled with rapture the sky is.
Somebody who feels deeply and loves poetry

had to have made all that! Imagine,
planning the sound of waves, how it would go on
for all eternity. Do you know that wonderful poem
by the Chinese poet Li Po, "Exile's Song,"
about friendship,
how it last throughout one's life, no matter
where it sends you? Will it be like that for us?
That poem is true! Sitting in San Diego,
you about to leave your home for places unknown,
our friend Michael's plans all in abeyance, and I
planning five permanent moves in the next month,
nothing now is closer to me than a memory
of us all getting kicked out of the Cotati Saloon
because we loved poetry
and wouldn't allow it to be insulted.
That, dear comrade, is what I call friendship.
Maybe we're all just here to thrust
the grace of past centuries,
preferably the romantic ones, into the great plastic jaws
of the video game of this present one.
Maybe we're here just to lay down an elegant cape
over some deep puddle, whether or not
anyone uses it to get across. Whatever the reason is,
I thank god for it. Running into all of you
has helped keep me on the right side of this century,
if there is one. And here in San Diego,
confronting this perfect beach, I think
how poorly this century fits me and yet
how comfortable I am in it, like clothes tailored
for another man that I've worn for a long time.
And I think how often I've hoped that just once,
a woman I barely know would hold those words of Yeats
that are always echoing around
the hollow caverns in my heart,
that she'd lean over, and murmur softly "how love fled,
and paced upon the mountains overhead,
and hid his face amid a crowd of stars."
                                        Love, Luke

Poem For Yannis Elias

Now the miracle comes.
Like the earth opening to each
drop of rain, our lives are opening.
The journey of the child
we planted together during the lonely summer
is almost done. Once more,
we are tasting the sweetness of life
in each cell of our bodies.
In a few hours, a small body
will be in our arms, inhabited
by all the secrets of the universe,
all the mysteries of time.
And we will listen to its first sounds
with humility, facing what every
mother and father have faced since the earliest times:
the small and simple spirit,
powerful, awesome, inexplicable.

A Small And Obscure Tribe

Near Placerville, off the freeway
and up into the hills, the government
is giving away two acres of land, free,
to any Indian belonging to
a small and obscure tribe.
Just about six families are there now.
One, an old woman and her children,
live in one of those sad trailers in which
you can see the rot setting
even while it's still in the showroom.
Her hair is white, she is heavy and smiles easily,
she could be almost anything,
but the children, with straight black hair
and beautiful olive complexions,
are clearly Indian. There are no lines for power,
no pipes or wells for water,

just the trailer, collapsed on the dirt
like a monstrous, dead toad.

I do not know this woman's past,
where she lived before,
how she came to accept this dubious half-gift,
made not from dignity or love, but rather
constructed piecemeal from the ugly guilt
buried deep in the nation's psyche,
and not so different, finally, from the trains
the Indians were herded into 100 years ago,
both of them just chains looped and draped
over a people who had walked
alone and free upon the earth.

A Sales Pitch

for Ace High

Dear Ace,

One thing you don't have in that little college town
you live in are ladies of the night.
We have them here.
Evenings leaving the Torch Club
sometimes they're three thick
on all the corners of 17th and L.
Well, it gives the cops something to do
to keep them out of real trouble.
Despite how all the people who live in the suburbs
say downtown's unsafe, there's remarkably little
for cops to do here. Most nights,
you see them in the all night greasy spoons,
or driving fast, sirens wailing down . . .
nothing, or flashing the razor of their searchlight
into the eyes of the corner ladies,
hassling them in an intimate, almost friendly way.
Everyone's used to it. There are worse,

more dangerous assignments, and the cops are grateful.
Parking my car the other night,
en route to last call at the Torch,
an older black prostitute noticed my bumper sticker.
"You a Yankee fan?"
"Life-long," I said. "Grew up in Yankee Stadium."
"Oh, yeah, baby, me too. I love them Yankees.
They goin' to win," she told me.
I thought about inviting her for a drink,
knowing what they'd think in the bar,
knowing it would be embarrassing for her
if they asked her to leave. But I wanted to talk to her
about the Yankees, about the cops, about her life.
Ace, it felt especially far from Cotati that night,
and I wondered what the distance is
between a nineteen year old college girl
and a black woman who has been selling herself
for who knows how long or why. We judge her.
I judge her. I judge her the next morning on my way
to my job for the Legislature, where some would sell
god and country to make sure they're reelected.
I'll bet she has children. Maybe some afternoons,
if the world has any justice, her old love, their father,
comes by. Maybe they stroll over to the park
and loll around in the hot sun,
the kids running through a sprinkler that's still on,
he and she lying quietly on the grass,
maybe thinking about how it was
when her belly started to bulge with the first of them,
back when the world was still a bell you could ring
if you were strong and brave enough.
Maybe she thinks, what a long journey it's been
from there to here. And who knows, maybe they came
all this distance because a few blocks away
in the Capitol, serious gray-suited men
negotiated with other gray-suited men
to find the highest price the earth would bring,
and had sold it to them, piece by piece, year after year.

Our Tribe

for Dawn and Bob on the Occasion of Their Marriage

The rain has owned our lives for months now.
What crops need to help them grow
has become their scourge. In our homes
we are surrounded by the excesses of nature
and of men, and we have begun
to lose our hope to fear of them.

On the news there is death and talk of death.
Some men promise us the next generation of weapons
will be the last we'll need to insure our security.
Small children burst awake in the middle of sleep
fear exploding in their brains.
Half the high-school children in America
believe they will die in a nuclear war.

Still, our tribe makes time to come together
to mourn the passing of a friend, or,
like now, to celebrate the joining of others.
Our children grow strong, lovely,
and, we hope, wise with compassion.
Thus, we find small ways to pluck life
out of the gray jaws of defeat, to let joy
be the blood that is rising
to flood-stage within our bodies.

Now, Bob and Dawn are the testament
to this oath of hope.
Today it is their beauty that holds fast
against those who build weapons
that kill our children.
We take these two into our lives,
for we have come here as much for us as for them,
and return to from where we came,
renewed, ready to do battle,
our tribe made whole again,
casting its light into the terrible darkness

where sirens wail
and searchlights sweep through the night.

Not Trying To Tell You About God

for John Fremont

There's always that person in each town
who reaches out to touch some of the lonely ones.
Not selfless, but he smiles to see
how his words keep reminding him that he cares,
and his face lights up when he sees how
what he said sprang up
like a guidepost in the dark road,
illuminated, pointing only
towards the little we can own.

He is not trying to tell you about god,
not a secret missionary holding a glittery
little piece of something in one hand
while the flyswatter poises in the air
just out of sight. But it makes him happy
to see some friend get smart,
even while he himself is fumbling around
the sweet secrets of his own life.

Letter To Tassia On Christmas

Dear Tassia,

Last night, Christmas eve,
I went to the local Catholic church
for midnight mass. No, I'm not converting,
but in a world of video games,
and cultural memories that seem to stretch back
maybe all of ten years,

I felt the need of something
that might be invisibly coiled
in the roots of our race.
I'm afraid for our world, old friend.
The bombs bursting in air isn't just a line
in a silly song anymore, but nightmarishly real,
and words from the current pontiff
have struck the only chord of sanity
in a world that seems mad for death.
But wherever the prince of peace was last night,
it was not that church, where the priest
must have had a late-night date,
he hurried so through the service.
And the highlight of the musical offering
was a sweet voiced woman singing
"The Little Drummer Boy." I sat in the church
after the service, alone, hoping for something
I cannot name, until the priest
began to look nervously at me,
some mad Irish bomber waiting to blow everything
to kingdom come. I walked out into the swirling rain
and thought how far poor Christ has come
from his first days in the stable in Bethlehem,
from his majestic presence in the works of Bach.
Maybe there is nothing left of history anymore.
The past has assumed all the importance
of a cancelled soap opera in the fall lineup.
Old agnostic I, I really do not know
how to pray, but if I did,
I'd get down on these knees and ask Jesus
to show us how to make the world reverberate again,
I'd ask for voices singing together
the old hymns, some ancient reverence
swelling up out of the collective human voice
to resonate in the shrines of grass
and the great tabernacles of wind.

Bringing Them Near

for Jonathan Raskin

There are nights when all your friends feel far.
You wander streets alone, grateful for lampposts,
their light sweeping over the silent sea of darkness,
watchtowers for humans, warning of shallows.
You think for a moment maybe you've spent
your forty years alone, wonder how you
could have come this far on so little gas.
Then, one by one, their faces spring up.
Little stories begin to sprout above the ground,
and suddenly someone you haven't thought of for years
is standing quietly inside your life.

Like Jonathan, dead now, one of those friends
you loved but hated sometimes too, because
he could do everything; fix cars, build houses,
then sit down and play Bach fugues on the guitar.
All the girls you wanted were wildly in love with him,
only spent time with you, you thought,
because he was busy and you were close.
He was cynical and hard and it finally killed him,
but oh, he could make you laugh.
He'd tell you the first thing to do
when you met a lady interested in you was,
"Get the keys." "To what?" you'd ask.
"Anything," he'd say. "The car. The house. Just
get the keys." Or he'd tell someone he'd just met,
as if reading from a fortune cookie,
"You will live a short
but miserable life." We laughed,
but that's just what he did, amid moments
of such tenderness that you'd have to redefine
the word "friend." Upward.

Let him go late at night
and other friends crop up, living and healthy
and easier to love. You recall you are still loved

by the woman who left you half a dozen times.
Suddenly each lamppost is a friend if you're still
out walking, the darkness between just journeys
you take to the home of each. If you stop in a bar,
you should know when you get home
you'll run your phone bill up,
plowing through that special address book
you never use except when you need to watch
small sparks of friendship
loom up out of the darkness.

There are nights when all your friends feel far.
Well, they are. But they can reach a thousand miles,
even from the grave,
to touch you. And they do.

On Receiving A Xeroxed Fundraising Letter From A Former Lover

for Hard Case

Months had gone by since I'd seen
that handwriting on an envelope:
your distinctive, handsome, no-nonsense scrawl.
Letters from you never fail
to fill me with gently nervous apprehension:
Have you left your husband?
Are you coming to Sacramento?
So I place it beneath the pile of bills, ads
and fundraising appeals, even beneath
the postcard from Hawaii and the letter
from a dear friend, and suddenly think the word "save,"
as in "save it for last,"
really has to do with
savoring. When I open it though,
it is a xeroxed appeal for funds
to help save the communal farm on which you live.
No note from you, not even the signature

that I own in such confusion in old boxes of letters,
is there to soften the twice-removed type.
Dutifully, I sit at my desk, open my checkbook.
I know how much this fight means to you.
And I care, not just because it is your home,
but because you are right.
But I think back over the years
that still stretch between us, that like leaves
dried after winter's soaking
are now curling up comfortably along their edges,
and see how often I had felt slighted by you
in ways we both know you did not intend.
How much damage was caused
by my nature, so easily bruised,
and the tough shell of yours
cannot be added like columns of figures.
Still, I wonder how different things might be now
if I had learned to hold my tongue
and not give voice to the sharp hurts
you could not know you wielded.
And sitting here in the quiet center
of this new storm of hurt,
I finally do that
which I had always failed to do
when it might have counted: look at what you mean.
This time, I see, it is not the letter,
but the envelope, how gently
you have placed my name on the pure whiteness
and planted the sad years between us
in the dark rows of these instructions of delivery:
from Albion; to Sacramento.
And the seasons
that have scattered us between them.

The Right Friend

for Patrick Grizzell

1

Oh, I wouldn't say it was the first time,
but I really lost my virginity one night at sixteen
in Nuevo Laredo on the third floor of an old hotel,
drunk on a quart of tequila that cost a dollar,
with my travelling companion and two whores
the front desk had sent up. They'd have,
we were assured, big tits.
They did. My friend and I lay on top of them
on twin beds separated by a couple of feet
of air so heavy and dank you could almost walk on it.
It was near dark in the room.
Outside, we could hear the laughter starting
on the street three thousand miles
from anything we knew,
the startlingly alive music insinuating itself
into everything. The two girls
talked in Spanish and giggled to each other
all during the time they were initiating us into
what we had been told were the pleasures of the flesh.
Done with us at last, dressed to leave, they said
we'd kept them late and charged us an extra dollar
for a taxi. In the room, we were alone, sober and quiet.
I picked up a towel one of the girls had dropped
and heard her giggling
deep in the memory of my bones.
My friend thought I was experienced in these matters,
and I knew he was not, and so we did not talk.
We didn't drink any more that night, either,
and in a few days we split up sadly
and went our separate ways, damaged and unhealed.

2

Twenty five years later, I finally have
the friend I should have been with that night.
In the darkness of that hotel room,
in the sudden starkness
of having made the perfunctory moves,
empty of love, we would have found a way
to turn the heat back up. Maybe it would have been
just another bottle of tequila, us drunk and laughing
about how silly and raunchy they'd been
that would have tilted the night upright again.
Or maybe we would have sat there in the dark,
shivering and silent, until one of us
had placed his arm gently around the other
in the profound assurance that love would still come,
would test us, and leave us, and come again,
that we would ache for it all our lives,
and that it would be our lot as men
to love women who laughed with each other
and spoke to each other
in languages we would never understand.

Last Of The Coffee

for Ben Hiatt

A lazy Saturday afternoon,
the heat rolling in
on the crests of small puffs of air.
The gold and white kitten,
too alive during the cool nights,
is curled asleep on the jeans
I spilled beer and wine on
during the poetry reading last night.
A beautiful Oriental girl, about sixteen,
goes by my window, little buds of desire
bursting open in the air around her.

Across the street, the good old boys
are drinking beer on the porch,
the bad rock and roll too loud,
while the two sparkling children
of one of them redeem the world.
I sit back drinking the last of this morning's coffee,
and read the good letter from my friend Hiatt again.
Now the cat springs down from the chair,
something at the open front door,
a fly on the screen probably,
catching her attention. I wonder
if the men with the bombs have ever spent a day
looking at the world this slowly;
how a girl walking by, or two children
shrieking in the grass, or the good words
of a friend, are the small flames
that set the right kind of fire to the earth.

Passing It On

for Yannis

My son, playing with a blond girl,
beautiful, his age,
suddenly loses his stubborn streak
to do her bidding.

Wisdom in the genes.

Playing The Game

Beautiful woman, blond, violet dress,
my favorite colors,
a seat away talking to friends
about baseball!
Perfume floats toward me
like a slow pop-up.
Old pro, I drift under it,
make it look easy.

Greenfield Ranch

for Susan Pepperwood

1.   Resources

Could I give it up?
Credit cards in the wallet?
Business cards in the jacket?
Turkey vulture floats over.
Wind ripples the pond.
No "resources" here — just trees,
grass, water, old friends.

2.   Feeding

"Perfect spot for my home,"
she thought a dozen years ago
          and here it is.
Flowers around,
big garden up the hill,
three acres fenced in
to keep out the deer.

And two deer beyond,
          a doe and her fawn,
finding food.

At The Flower Stand

for Ace High

1.   Drive On

Little breeze brings the scent of
last remaining carnations
up to my nostrils.
Orange Toyota truck,
two men look us over,
drive on.
Flowers, me,
breath sighs of relief.

2.   Strawberries

Beautiful blond woman,
          small Chevy pickup.
Driver some lout
          with a CAT cap—
No strawberries and wine
          for her tonight.

The Unofficial Poem Of
The 1984 Summer Olympics

These Olympic gymnasts,
tiny even on TV
where everything is diminutive,
conquer hearts as well as gold
with that pure beauty
we poets love to prove is false.
I'd ply Julianne McNamara
with magnums of champagne,
make her listen to her first jazz,
peel that skin-tight leotard off her
star by star by stripe.

A Saint Francis Hotel Poem

for Norman Mailer

Well, ok, but outside this interior window
it could almost be New York,
Lower East Side, Puerto Ricans yelling
across the courtyard, whatever the hour.
The rears of those old tenements
that hid backyards, a few thin trees,
sometimes even a garden,
were what we knew of the land.
It was a different world
from the rude streets in front:
slower, intimate, sexy,
the mad array of the smells of dinners cooking
all over the world crammed there
in that one small space; and, oh, the languages,
Spanish, Portuguese, Hungarian, Polish, Russian,
even the German sounded good
those soft summer evenings.

I'm so far from that life now
I thought of it for the first time in twenty years
tonight, in the exclusive Saint Francis Hotel,
in San Francisco, at the age of forty-one.
Then, in my twenties, on East Seventh Street
in a seven room flat, I had once even let
the romance of clotheslines, of sheets slowly spiraling
in an evening breeze off the East River
lure me into the arms of poetry, into some way
a young man who could not afford a camera
could snap it pure and right and nail it down.

It's Friday Night — The Sequel

It's Friday night. Your friends have all escaped town
for the weekend. Your room-mate's with his lady,
and what had recently seemed
an excess of woman friends
has suddenly without your knowing how
shrunk into none. One possible liaison is delayed
by dense complications with a former lover,
another has decided two's more difficult for her
than she'd thought it'd be, and the choice was simple:
one the easy, long history; the other your flimsy excuse
for being so half-there. It's Friday night
and you're not getting any younger, kiddo.
In the old days, you'd have hit the bars alone,
staggered home hours later, a little drunk,
that sweet melancholy inebriation sometimes brings,
a couple of phone numbers on matchbooks
so exhilarating it won't matter when they don't pan out.
But mornings after are as old as you are,
so you try to choose
between a movie, a book, or blues on the stereo,
settle for a glass of wine on the front porch,
wait for the phone to ring,
or the party to start across the street
they come over and invite you to,
the hostess a beautiful woman who left her husband
a year ago because she grew tired of the silence
and was just telling her best girlfriend
she thinks she's ready to meet someone new.
You walk across the street in your best faded jeans,
a bottle of good wine in one hand,
the other opening and closing,
clutching at the emptiness.

A Poem To Explain The Need For The Way Up, Firm & High Tail It Bright Out Of Town Detective Agency's Annual Bacchanalia Softball Game And Then Some

for Fair Warning

Dear Gary,

The 49ers won it today.
As reluctant a fan as I am,
Montana's poise and grace moved me.
In the bars, though, the grace of the game
escapes those who cheer them on.
These people are not pretty
and it helps to remind me why I love baseball
and basically zero out during football season.
In Europe, older and wiser than us,
football is soccer, a game which, like baseball,
leaves the door to heroism open to each player,
no matter his position. I like that.
I like it that players known for their great
fielding ability suddenly erupt for
three homeruns and a double
in some World Series game.
It means the rest of us
have a chance. We get the great looking girl
every now and then, have a kid
the likes of whom the world has never seen,
or win the sweepstakes and take off for the tropics.
Somewhere in the world, Gary,
I have a half-brother and sister
their mother has hidden away from me,
progeny nevertheless
of that gray, wiry-haired old author at whom
Hemingway once wrote, "Harvey, you write good."
Do they know that? Does she tell them?
Does she let them know that their father was
an old bohemian, roaming around the country
during the Depression with Kenneth Patchen?

Well, old friend, I've taken you a long way,
from the Super Bowl champs to literary talk,
but we have sons, same age more or less,
and far enough away from our golden age
that we have to plot their indoctrination.
It won't be easy. They've never seen
DiMaggio slice a bad one into the seats,
or listened to Lauren Bacall whistle. Gary,
I hope we keep the games going that long.
Tonight, Super Bowl Sunday, I finally realized
the answer to the question the uninitiated always ask:
"Why the Agency? Is it a joke?"
Now I know: to keep the game alive,
for the children. For the children.

New Poems

Sacramento, California
1987 - 1989

Zihuatanejo

for Felicita

Cove of two suns, two moons,
of this paradise for wealthy travellers,
this sad land of poverty,
on whose beaches mingle the fair and dark skins
of two destinies, one the cool marble of banks,
the other the dark earth of the fields,
on whose soft, feminine roads
roam *bandidos* with *pistoles,*
their powder mixed with one part hunger,
one part fear, one part a hostility
caused by this love affair with us
they must have and do not want.

Cove of two suns, two moons,
on whose hilltop sits
the sprawling, unfinished mansion
built by "The General,"
the corrupt police chief of Mexico City,
whose children are in school in Canada
hauled through the air in steel carts, whose harness is
pulled taut against the shoulders of their people,
on whose beaches I drink tropical fruit drinks
while translating Neruda, who died of a broken heart
twenty-one days after his country was murdered
by the CIA,
in whose waters perch massive tour boats,
their spotlights cast eerily over dancers, over water,
over a beach whose last inhabitant is a cow,
come down for the salt in the water.

Cove of two suns, two moons,
above which daily soar the jetliners,
taking off from the lush jungles of Zihuatanejo
with their drinks and bad food,
whose pressurized interior is the paddywagon
returning us to the cell of *Los Estados Unidos,*

where robbery often does not come
on a curved and lush roadside, two men
brandishing *pistoles*,
and often does not come for the same reasons.

Cove of two sun, two moons,
with your waters of azure,
your lush fruit and the smell everywhere
of fresh tortillas and beans,
with your earth resonating with ancient reverence,
your fishing boats in the harbor and men
drinking *cerveza* at the stands of stone terraces,
your pelicans which no longer come,
your markets of endless bowls and pants
and sandals and dust, your long lines
of food stalls and children,
your movie houses crumbling and archaic,
your bookstore with one copy of Neruda in Spanish,
your pretty shopgirl teaching Spanish phrases
to my friend, practically weightless with love.

Cove of two sun, two moons,
where lightning is like a pane of brilliant glass
against the sky all night,
where dawn rises up from the sea in soft leaps of foam,
hold me hard against this dark loam of earth
so I may again be of it when I swoop heavy
out of the skies into that colder place of home.

Letter To Cole Swensen From Zihuatanejo

*"I only wish I'd studied Latin more in school
so I could have understood more."*
          Vice President Dan Quayle,
          commenting on his trip to Latin America.

Dear Cole,

Finally back in a country that respects its poets, lying on
the beach, knowing how deep
words have been spoken here.
A few months ago, an article on the front page of
the Sunday New York Times Magazine
told of how Latin American governments
parade their new policies past their poets and writers
before unveiling them publicly, to make sure they will be
acceptable to beloved poets and thus to the people.
Small wonder,
in countries where children strew flowers in the paths
of their great poets,
where the poets are ambassadors to other nations
or where, like now in Nicaragua,
made part of the government itself.
Imagine Reagan calling Gary Snyder, saying,
"Gary, let me run this new welfare idea by you,"
and Snyder saying, "Just a minute, Ron, let me finish
the line I'm working on." No, as we know too well,
in the U.S. poets suffer neither prison or castigation,
just the profound indifference of benign neglect.
Meanwhile, the language atrophies and dies. Politicians
think the schools don't teach enough math and science
while the children themselves have no language left
to let us know of their screaming inside, sick with
the cancers of television and fast food. Your work
with Poets-In-The-Schools has taught you
how doors are opened
for the kids by teaching them the language of the heart.
So I send you in this aerogram
the Mexico of my soul,

this land where the hills are soaked in language,
in nuance, in subtlety,
where the beauty of the spoken word
has not been diminished by television's homogenization,
and where words are not stricken from the vocabulary
because some group finds them offensive;
I send you the desire I have to know this language again,
this language of Neruda and Lorca,
of Vallejo and Hernandez,
of Paz, Marquez and Borges, and more,
I send you what I wish
every poet in our nation could have,
what every Latin American poet has always known,
the knowledge of how crucial it is to keep thrusting
the language of truth into the jaws
of the language of deception,
to make each word resound with dignity and strength,
to hold up the sky with these pillars of human sound.

Passing The Morning

I wonder what everybody's doing this morning?
Hiatt in Folsom, a beer already maybe?
Probably just coffee, he's got a printing job today,
best not to start in on the brew too early.
Poems flying off the press soon,
all that ink churning into beauty,
all that silent paper filling up with sound,
all the truth in the air like that commercial
a white tornado funnelling down into Hiatt's study.

Grizzell, he doesn't take too long in the bathroom now
with his beard, down to his last few days
in the house he and Theresa have loved in for years,
about to move in here with me, my compañero.
Still, I worry about little beard hairs in the sink.
He worked on poems last night in the kitchen,
kids and woman asleep, the light yellow on the page,

refrigerator buzzing, him crouched over the table,
in his hands that pen
he can make do so many things.
If he were oriental he'd be delicate
haiku brush painter instead of clumsy old American
having to spend his time hanging out in bars with me,
searching for women who love poetry,
or at least don't mind it.

Ace, no question about it,
he's got new Rolling Stones' *Under Cover Of The Night*
loud spinning, could he be alone?
Prancing around his house, surrealist microphone
in hand, a glass doorknob
wrapped in black furlined glove,
he'll have to sell flowers in inclement weather today,
he'll soon be excited about new never read before
surrealist poem, wait all day anxiously to call me
and read it, wait all the long hours he cannot leave
his flower stand, The Reincarnation Station, and me
with my phone not put in yet anyway.

I wonder if Sean, now that he's getting married,
still pours himself a shot of brandy for his coffee,
Senior Partner Chow we call it, a great recipe
handed down from one generation of floozies
to the next.

Les probably already out building a house.
Eyes so clear and blue eagles mistake them for the sky.

Mary Rose has woken up feeling so good about herself
she is waltzing around her living room
to the soft strains of Nat "King" Cole, wondering why
sometimes it's hard to be alone,

while across town Robyn, her beautiful red-gold hair
rising over the horizon of her brow,
stands absentmindedly
trying to remember the details of a dream she just had
in which she understood everything.

And I,
oh I am just in my new home,
third cup of coffee, trying to fulfill my promise
to myself to write three poems before food,
wondering what it would be like
if all of you weren't out there,
if it were just the presidents and premiers,
their cold, metallic toys
in precise, deadly little rows,
aimed at these human cities,
at the back alleys of sorrow
and the great slums of joy.

Information

for Dee

"I cannot give out information.
Please understand my position,"
you tell me. Yet,
the clear, crisp hand
in which you write to me,
the undulating fall
of the single braid
down the long perfection
of your bronzed back,
the authority with which you move
through this domain
of hotel sterility
and lonely travelers,
the powerful odor of your suspicion,

all these are messages
trailing after you
as clear as the spoor
a lion leaves
moving with feline and fearless grace

down the trail she owns,

information you are giving out
as beautiful and indifferent
as the messages of light
the moon sometimes leaves
on the bare skin of the sea.

White Christmas

Christmas.
Snow covers much of the world.
Even the generals pad softly along.

Real Ideology

for Amnesty International

The claims of justice all governments make,
right or left,
end where forests open up
onto the clearings of small villages
late at night.
The cries of children
suddenly separated
by uniformed, sneering men
from their fathers
is translated by governments into,
"The happy people."

My old English teacher told me
a poet was being sloppy
if he wrote about the plurals of things,
that our job
is precision: focus on the one.
In this poem, though,

there are too many for that:
too many disappeared in Argentina;
too many shot at night in Salvadoran towns
brilliant with searchlights;
too many forgotten in Siberia
or the new prisons the Soviets call
mental institutions; too many native women
permanently sterilized by Peace Corps doctors.

It is not ideology.
It has never been ideology.
It is men
clinging to the power that rises to them
from the piles of bleached bones
and the screams of children
the wind is made to carry.

Why Write?

for Susan Hofberg

On my wall, a Steinberg drawing
from an old New Yorker cover: the word
"Today" in brilliant orange-red,
blue peacock plumes of fire
blasting it off rocket-like
from the launch pad of "Yesterday."
Above, because like poets
artists think they can see the future,
the future arc of the rocket:
" . . . Breakfast . . . Lunch . . . Dinner . . .
Tomorrow." I love this drawing enough
that I searched two years
to finally find it under my nose
and stole it off the copy in the state library,
never missed (at least until this poem),
thus lending a certain truth
to its obvious implication:

although there is a vast blue sky,
there is no room for god in this drawing.
There are other, smaller things left out as well:
between breakfast and lunch,
coffee and work; same for after lunch.
This season's television creations
neatly and exactly fit
the space between dinner and tomorrow.
Even Johnny Carson doesn't have to be left out.
Steinberg has thus captured
the vastness of the meaning of life.
Some of us poets sit quietly at home,
before dinner, after the ballgame,
sketching in the details.

Bob Dylan Sings About The Redwoods

After years of angry remonstrations
about our lack of faith in Jesus,
Dylan finally looks around again
and gets it.
"Trust yourself," he sings.

It's Saturday afternoon.
Two days ago, the California state budget emerged
from its sticky cocoon.
Buried in its fat folds of money,
quiet, trying to attract little attention,
lie seven million dollars
to take into the kindred silence of the wilderness
a few hundred acres of giant, ancient redwoods.
A veto is expected: there are men
who want to rape these survivors,
these tall women with their pleated, green skirts,
and our governor may act to make it legal.

Somewhere in the north woods, a chain saw
sees first light glancing in

through the cracks of the tool shed.
Feels in the last darkness the sharp sparks of death
its teeth can make, and rubs them
like a cat along the old wooden frame.

A small band of us will see this through.
It cannot be that after ten years of struggle
we can have gotten this far
only to fail.
But Dylan is back. God is dead.
We can trust ourselves again. Nothing is certain,
certainly not death or taxes. Ask the forests.
And time is not, after all, money.

Investigation

"Elementary, my dear Watson."
The line Sherlock Holmes never says.

It is late Sunday evening.
You are gone, deep by now in the sleep you cannot get
when we are sheet-tangled together.
Public radio is playing piano blues.
I'm drinking the second to last glass of champagne
in the bottle we opened together. I'll drink the last
before bed — it's no good
when the bubbles go, even though
I don't know why they go
or where. Sunday night is a good time
for deep questions about bubbles and sleep,
for making love on the living room floor,
for drinking champagne,
because Sunday night is always
the closest we come to death
until death. There is physical evidence for this.
More people die early Monday morning
than any other time of the week.
After three million years, even the skeptics among us

concede that this is more than just chance.
Doctors think it's because
people drink and party too hard over the weekend,
and psychologists think it's because
Sunday night is the time when we are forced to confront
the emptiness of our fantasies, etc.
But poets . . .
ahh, poets know it is joy that kills us.
So if I die this morning, send the police
on a wild goose chase. Don't tell them
about our night together,
how you sat on me on the floor
and we talked together about the deep spots
we kept discovering in each other
as we rode the wild night.
Just tell them that you left,
let them think you left me in despair.
And whatever you do, don't go down to Baker Street,
don't let Holmes take his magnifying glass
to the carpet, or to the towels with which
we cleaned each other afterwards,
or to my skin which would still hold your scent
the way dying roses hold onto
that which the earth has bathed them in.
Because even if you took care to clean it all,
if you hid every clue, still the great Holmes
would know that I had died of joy, not sorrow,
for there are traces throughout this apartment
not even you could find,
traces that tell the tale of how, after you left,
I poured more champagne
and danced around the room,
leaving small particles of joy clinging
to each bit of air, clues so small
that Inspector Lestrade would be once again confounded,
but clues nonetheless
left from one great detective to another.

The Outhouse

for Nancy

Among the many remarkable things you have done,
the outhouse shines. First morning
I wake with you, I walk out
onto the soaking grass, naked
but for the white, button-down shirt,
last vestige of civilization — what I do out there —
and climb the few steps to the small wooden shelter,
protected from the bad weather
this mountain is known to summon,
but one wall not built, naked to the east,
or should I say, The East, this strange dharma
of Greenfield Mountain. I sit
on the comfortably padded seat,
no stranger to civilization yourself,
and watch the sun slanting down on the far ridge
where now I see that four horses have come out
to graze on the sweet grasses that grow
only at the edge of the world.
When I return to the bed, and you open your arms
to heat my chill, I shudder at your touch
the way horses shudder, their skin
moving like the tide above their blood,
and I grip you in a new way,
wilder and move alive than when I left.

Stealing Watermelons

How could I suddenly remember a night
almost forty years ago, stealing watermelons
from the sheriff's backyard in Cranbury, New Jersey,
after all that's happened? Bobby and I
crawled along the darkened fences
that were there to keep,
after the lights in the houses would go dark,
the yards and planted fields
from soaring off into the night.
We trusted those fences enough
that we were sure the watermelon field
we searched for had stayed put.
There were many watermelon fields in that town —
it would be easy to say
we decided on the sheriff's because
it was closest to the small two-boy tent
our kind and patient parents had said
could contain our huge and limitless lives
that night at least. I like to think
it was instead as Lou Lipsitz wrote,
that a tribe of Indians of which he had read
dug the clay for their pipes
only on the land of their enemies —
they said only those pipes were real.
Those watermelons came easy out of the ground
as if they longed to be with us
until a beam of light flashed
from the sheriff's door and the voice
that had warned school assemblies
called out into the black night,
"Come out or I'll shoot!"
Perhaps for boys, the fear of being hauled
before your mother is greater than that
of being shot,
for we did not come out,
we ran, crouching along
the fences and dark hedges,
clutching our precious contraband,

terrified but, as young boys will
who believe they can never die,
laughing uproariously
as we tore up the soft earth with our flashing feet.
Back in the tent, we bit into
the sweetest watermelon we had ever tasted.
We ate, and dribbled,
and hugged each other in admiration
for our bravery, and in that holding discovered
our first real sexual stirrings.
In all the myriad years gone by
since that simple night when the night shone down
on our innocence, I have never
desired to be with a man. But flush with fruit
and its sensuous juices, we tried to enter
each other that night,
our little cocks hard against each other.
I do not think we succeeded much.
We must have given it up,
and in our spent energy
finally turned from each other
into the more familiar comfort of sleep,
and slept to the end of our friendship.
When the glare of morning hit the tent flaps,
I said good-bye fast, not thinking why.
From then on in school, I was barely polite.
He never asked why. I do not remember
his last name, or how his father
earned their keep, or even if
his mother was fair.
But we had dug clay for a pipe
on the land of our enemy, and had held each other
hard on the hard earth, and had given each other
what love we could
before the sunlight came and snapped away
the dark's hard-earned, lovely wisdom.

Dealing With Fog

for Sean Kilty

Dear Sean,

You go through high school wondering what it means,
English class after English class
   "the winter of our discontent." Now,
in your fourth decade, you know. Fog and gray skies
hang over the valley and Sacramento is England
without the bawdiness we'd hoped
or even the buildings of Parliament.
We have the Capitol,
but despite the speeches of politicians,
we all know no empire was ever launched from here,
no epic religious wars, brave lads sent out
to convert the heathens.
Yesterday afternoon, the sun broke through.
I was in my office.
I put down the papers and just looked out the window.
Below, in Capitol Park, the mood shifted. Trees
from every forest in the state suddenly reappeared,
their green name tags.
A woman in tight jeans strode purposefully by,
and I was suddenly lost in a dream of sun and lust,
those elements which no chemistry teacher
ever managed to convince me
were not the building blocks of life.
If we'd had Ace High
teaching Chemistry 101
we wouldn't have had to spend all this time
beating around the bush.
If you'll pardon the more or less
unintentional pun.
I know you're wondering what this poem is about, Kilty,
but look back up top and you'll see
it's just a letter to you,
rambling on about this and that, the Reader's Digest
condensed version of my life. Nancy called today

and said, it's ok, we're friends forever.
My mother gets stronger in New York
and my sister's baby, Kate, approaches her first birthday.
I will not attend. First birthday parties are
notoriously boring. People drink milk.
Kate will still be unable to talk seriously about
Proust's *Swann's Way*
or even the latest trendy critic's view
that Kerouac's body of work
was that of a frustrated and latent pianist
who could only afford the keys on an old Royal.
Old pal, it's late Friday night and you'd be proud of me,
snifter of brandy on the desk, Bach on the phono,
and the phone unlikely to ring.
We're alone in here once again,
you and I, despite how your wife Ann may think
that at this very moment
she has her arms wrapped tightly about you. We are,
after all, very sideways characters,
and, to borrow the ancient Kerouackian approach,
we are packing the rods of eternity,
great detectives of the void
in the perfect starry dynamo of sitdown night.
It's late. Arthur Grumiaux has just
done something to Bach on the violin
every music teacher insists cannot be done.
Garcia Lorca is preparing to enter the public schools
despite the fact they will not give him tenure.
There is nothing to do now except wait for morning,
wait for the sun to lift
each cup of fog to its lips and drink.

Baseball As Life: Metaphor Number Three

When they finally let me in the game,
late in an inning where appearances
by second stringers could neither lift or sink
the team, I surprised them all
and hit a clean single over the shortstop's head
into left field. The sun was shining
I suddenly noticed, as, thirteen years old,
I raced to first and made the big turn, professional,
to draw a throw. I stepped back onto first,
trying not to look around at my team-mates
to see their surprised congratulations,
one of them at last.
I watched the pitcher
kick dirt on the mount, and took my lead.
The first baseman walked nonchalantly toward me
and tagged me with the ball
he had hidden in his glove.
"Out!" the infield umpire hollered.
I looked around for a moment
for a higher authority to which one could appeal —
it was my first hit in my first game,
a moment of glory; somewhere in the rules
it must say no such moment can turn to shame —
but there was no higher authority of fairness
to turn to, only laughter from their dugout,
embarrassed silence from ours.
I walked back to the bench,
the last place on earth I wanted to be,
but choiceless,
believing as crushed children do
that the end of the world had arrived.
It had. For years,
even as I watched it arc from other first basemen
back to other pitchers, I feared that ball
always in his glove,
and he always the same, a little older,
bigger, more handsome than me.
I hate him I guess, and I owe him too.

For even as I am counted "success"
in the world's arithmetic,
even as these poems have forced
blank paper to occasionally take a bow,
even though more women have loved me
than first stirrings ever thought would bring,
there is always near me
the first baseman. He is handsome and strong.
They want him for the cheesecake calendar.
Girls in the stands pass phone numbers to guards.
He has tricks no one like us
has ever imagined. Whatever we do,
no matter how clean the hit,
how short the lead,
how clear the throw back to the mound,
when you lead off first,
the ball will be there, in his mitt,
holding you firmly to the earth.

Bourbon By The Bed

for My Mother

Dear Mother,

I'm writing to you late on a Sunday afternoon,
already ninety-five degrees at six o'clock
and we're barely into April. There's an orange tree
just outside my window, the fruit, heavy with juice,
pulling the thin branches it owns toward the earth.
There is no sign of city. I could step out this back door
and emerge, as in Narnia, into the coastal county
where my children live. Almost. Really, though,
they're four hours in a car,
you and my sister five in a plane.
I didn't plan any of this. I never meant to be
so far from everyone. If I had one wish it'd be
to shrink the country so we could all live where we like,

step out the back door into the garden and
call to each other over the wall. Oh well,
no wee Irish Leprechaun today, his three wishes
brimming with humor.
The loneliness I once thought romantic
turned out to be just aloneness after all,
and too many poets have said it too well. I don't know
what the critics would say
about ending a poem with a joke,
but they say if you don't drink,
don't eat meat, don't smoke
and don't make love, you'll live longer.
It's not true, mother, keep your cigarettes handy
and the bourbon by the bed,
and if some sweet man comes along,
go on, sing him into your bed.
You won't live longer if you don't —
it will just seem longer.
The void out there we all must enter has time enough —
a few days or even years won't shrink it much.
I intend to swagger to its door drunk, the money spent,
taking with me, if I can, only the memory
of all the sweet arms, including yours,
that held me for a time against the long dark.

The Severing Of The Roots

for Steve Tropp

You hang on in the most tenuous ways,
grabbing at the earth,
trying not to see the graves they're in.
If you don't die first in some strange, accidental way,
you're going to get cut off from them,
those roots of yours,
going to be left there suspended in the air,
going to be without the elders of your tribe.

My father sat on the edge of the bed watching
the funeral of Martin Luther King when
he slid down to the floor, swooning and lost.
The woman he was learning to love (after
the mothers of all his children had drifted off like
the smoke from the cigarettes that hung loosely
from his lips whenever he gazed
at the page in the typewriter) called out, "Harvey!" and
with the last light fleeing the vacancy of his eyes he
managed to croak, "What?"
the last word ever from this man of words,
a word hurled at the blackness,
a word grasping at understanding.

Now I feel the knife digging into this last other root,
rummaging around under the earth
where my feet are planted,
trying to sever the life from my mother.
A bad fall two years ago,
the hip never mending, the heart attack last summer,
the perpetual drinking as if her life were already over,
finally at eighty-four having to give up the class
she teaches at the university
because she remembers for a second
how much she perpetually forgets.

Above me, the world is emptying.

Below, my own children feel how I instinctively dig deep
into the ground for their sustenance,
to be the one root that belongs to them.
My three-year old daughter said to no one in particular,
gleefully, "My daddy's hair is gray," the word gray
said as if it was a merry little song.
Forgive me, I'm not sure what I'm writing about.
There's some connection I'm trying to make, something
that I think you need to know, about me, about life.
My friend's mother died two days ago,
without warning, in Victoria Station, London.
The trains must have been growing suddenly silent.

Friends, I'm holding out these hands.
They've been filled and emptied so many times and
I can't remember what with.

A Life

for My Mother On Mother's Day

As I hang up the phone after talking with you,
after your sobs had grown slowly more punctuated,
after you had tried to hide the lack of control
you had just displayed to your son whose hair is gray
but who is still your child,
I imagine your weeping breaking out
all over again, contained at first, then
uncontrollable, your heart breaking,
as your memory, which cannot even hold the taste
of dinner with your daughter last night, churns up again
for the millionth time how,
for most of your eighty-four years,
you had, while disdaining feminism,
struck out on a most independent course.
With no college, you had two children
with the man you loved above all others,
while nevertheless avoiding marriage,

and brought unheard of authors
to American audiences through your unlikely job
as literary editor of Harpers Bazaar, winning the award
three years running for publishing the best short story
to appear in the nation. Sung by Roethke
for publishing his poems and sending him money,
my father gave you children
and fifteen years of his life for publishing his.
And even after the Hearst Corporation's
mandatory retirement twenty years ago
("If we make an exception in your case, Miss Morris,
we'll have to do it for everybody."),
you managed to start a whole new career
as a teacher of the short story at The New School,
your class over-subscribed each year
until now. Is there a time when things suddenly change
and begin some unplanned and awful descent?
Could we graph your life from the fall on the ice
in front of your home in Greenwich Village,
your hip never mending,
forced to a cane and then to a walker? For the first time,
mortality had shoved its ugly face in yours
and made you question how far you could go on.
Your house in Maine that you loved
above all your possessions,
suddenly was a thousand miles further away.
Then, last summer, the heart attack
that you did not recognize
and still to this day do not believe,
the panicked phone calls from coast to coast,
the final return to New York —
I visited you after you came home from the hospital,
do you remember?
We talked and laughed and I made myself believe
you were really coming around,
would teach again in the winter.
Now, another six months has gone by.
When I call you at noon
you're already drunk. You do not remember my age,
are surprised when I tell you my hair

has gone quite gray.
"I don't believe it," you sing into the phone,
almost happily, like a little girl,
like my young daughter who you have never met,
and yet whom you are growing more strangely like.
Your daughter has become the monster in your life,
denying you liquor even as she hates doing it,
because the doctors say it will shorten your years.
And like her,
although without the immediacy of responsibility,
I share her reluctance
to increase the number of your years,
the long years through which you will have no trouble
looking further back and recalling who you were
and will never be again.
Oh, I would buy you whiskey, mother,
to spare you that pain, to spare you
your weeping, out of control,
down at the bottom of the well
into whose mouth we have all climbed,
and from which there is no return ever, even for you.
I end here, because poems, like lives,
must end somewhere.
Except to say that while it is lovely to think of you
when you were young,
when you held your young son high in the air
to teach him stars
and the fragrance of your rich brown hair,
I am also finding the loveliness of you now
as you grow in these disparate directions:
yes, toward the inevitability of the grave;
but more, at your strangely gleeful moments,
into the sweet innocence of my daughter,
who is of your flesh, your blood,
your wisdom and bravery,
your sweetness, your love and mine.

Children Without Food

It is the haunted look in their eyes
that binds us to the evening news,
those children without food in Ethiopia
or Appalachia, those people without homes
in Bangladesh or New York,
those old people who built the nation
and have been reduced to counting pennies.

I have seen also
the faces of the men who live
in the deep caverns with the bombs. In their eyes
there is a look of vacancy: the tenants gone,
the place in disrepair, their only occupant
the empty passage of time.
Money flows down to them, alone there
in the caverns with their gleaming steel,
these musicians ready to play the chord of death
on the final synthesizer before them.
Money burrows down to them
like a rat through the floor of Congress
into the rotting caverns,
where it gnaws on the shredding line
that ties us to the planet.

It is said in the Oval Office where the president speaks
that this money burrowing down into the dank caverns
will protect us from the menace
beyond our borders, our seas.
That all this gleaming steel strikes fear into those
who would conquer and own this nation.

I think the money does this,
protects us from the enemy beyond,
puts our nation beyond their reach.
They too have seen the haunted eyes of our children,
our homeless masses huddled under bridges,
the indifference with which we treat our elderly.
Once they may have seen America

as some great prize, gleaming and modern and sleek.
But now they have looked more closely.
They have their own mouths to feed.

So. It's done. The policy worked. We can stop now.
The enemy is busy, looking to its own needs.
It is time to go down into the caverns
and get back the money.
Buy some food for the children, build some homes
for those who wander our streets,
open the hospital doors for those who are sick.
Become America again.

But what if we don't? What if
we have believed in the missiles for so long
that we can't say no? What if
we're addicted to missiles and bombs?
What if instead of homes, we build only bomb shelters?
if instead of food, we grow only reactors?
if instead of healing the ill,
we correct only for function and drive?

All those men are trapped in the deep caverns
beneath the earth now, clutching their money.
We are above them, digging into the earth
with our simple tools of truth.
We will break through any time now.
The sun is cresting the horizon
and is about to blaze up around
the steel towers and the steel men
and bring them visible into the light.

Jenner

Where the river meets the sea, a town.
Its addresses rise up the steep incline
from the low confluence
to the cliffs that sing above the fog,
somehow measuring the scales of the lives
the town has found a way to own.
Once, traveling
with a woman I loved,
I found a room riverward
and below the town
and awoke to a morning
that had swum upstream towards us
from the beginning of time.
Gulls and a lone osprey rose out
of the primordial mist
hanging like a fragrance above the river.
Away to our right, we could see the churn
of water meeting water,
and the sun dappling the high leaves
of the trees that hugged the banks.
We changed our plans for breakfast
and made coffee in the little electric pot.
We stood on the small, awkward terrace,
its paint gone, gone with the damp seasons,
and watched the steam from our coffee
drift up into the clear air,
watched the birds dive golden in the sun
out of the soft winds
towards any breakfast the river might release,
watched the land and water separate in light,
and almost believed
that we had invented, if not love,
then at least coffee,
a million years before its time.

Poem For Francisco Mendes

They killed the earth in Brazil yesterday.
They hired a man who had a gun.
He came to Brazil and found the earth.
There were other men who were paid
to protect the earth from the man with the gun
and the men with the money
to give the man with the gun.
But I guess they were not paid enough.
In any case, the earth was already weakened.
Ordinarily, it would have been easy
for the earth to stop him.
.But the trees were gone, the earth's lungs.
And the air was so clogged with smoke and waste
that the earth could not smell.
And the water was so foul
that the earth could not clear itself.
Plus, you know, the earth was looking
for its birds, that were gone,
it was looking for its fish, that were poisoned,
it was looking for its children,
but they were inside, watching television.
It was looking for the beautiful men and women
who had promised to treasure it,
but they were hiding out since the election.
So the earth was busy
and maybe was even despairing a little
when the man with the gun
who had been given the money
came to kill the earth.
After the earth was dead, Time Magazine
said that the earth was the Man of the Year.
After the earth was dead, George Bush
said that he was an environmentalist
and that he would save it.
After the earth was dead, the police caught the man
with the gun who had been given the money.
"I killed Francisco Mendes," he told them.
But it was not true.

They had sent him to kill a man,
and what he had done was to kill the earth.

Lodi

Right off, she's there in the liquor store
with her two kids, tight jeans, naturally
curly brown hair, sweet smile . . .
husband out in the pickup? Or single,
bringing them up herself?
Here with friends to give a poetry reading,
I dream the simple life of Lodi for a second,
dream of settling into a small house
on the country side of town,
barbecues and baseball, PTA
and the annual neighborhood meeting
about the loud music from the new tenants
or the planned development that'll wreck everything.

Am I really going to miss all this? Never
just a simple guy, better to her than anyone
because three or four poems a year
keep me sensitive? Oh, I'd be the town radical,
stirring up trouble and embarrassing her, probably
the reporter for the Lodi Sentinel digging
to find where that city councilman got the money
for the '84 Lincoln Continental,
but still be friends with the deputies.

In Lodi, someone at the reading said,
Sacramento's the cultural mecca. We visitors laughed,
looking west to San Francisco with similar awe.
But what if concerts were once a year
and poetry readings special occasions
when you bundle up the kids
and pack them in the back of the pickup, what then?
Glowing with passion because
a few poets from Sacramento

had opened the night with language,
we'd get home late,
our dog barking until she knew it was us,
sit in the truck for a minute in the silence
that had rushed in when the engine shut down
to not disturb the spell . . .

And they, in their own car,
hurtling over the dark miles to home,
wondering about us, our deep silences,
our flat miles of fields and fertilizer, our bad poetry
and the awesome joy in which it bathes us.

Messages

for Terri Carbaugh & Mary Rose Sullivan--
& my father, who'd have loved them both

I stand on the corner outside the Hofbrau
not wanting to go home,
not wanting to go in, thinking
maybe a friend will come by.
Each time the door closes,
a deep cloth is spread out over the music,
softening those hard blues the way I need.
The cool night breeze comes up
and even though I have not been inside
with the smoke and the sweat, it feels good.
A pretty but timeworn blond
comes up 17th Street and says hi to me. "Hi," I say back.
She stops and inspects me for a minute.
"Well," she says kindly, "what's happening?"
"Oh, just waitin' for a friend.'
She smiles. "I'm pretty friendly."
"Well, I'm pretty broke," I tell her.
"Another time," she says, and turns the corner
onto the street of sorrow, the street of hope . . .

Well, it's really just J Street. It must be those blues again,
that poetry reading earlier,
romanticizing things. It must be how everyone I love
is somewhere else, how empty my house is about to be,
how I hope for messages
even when it's too late to return the call.
When I get home, a friend has come through,
patiently waited for the beep and said,
call me when you can.

Oh, I'd call at one in the morning,
wake you from your sleep,
force you to disentangle yourself
from the arms and legs of your lover,
just to hear your voice, your deep laugh,
the conversation made intimate by the hour
and the silent proximity of your bedmate.
Through this wire, I have crossed the city and
stepped into your boudoir
and unbuttoned the intimate apparel of sleep.

But I don't. Instead, I turn on KJAZ,
I pour a drink, I approach this old Royal,
I write these words. I feel good.
In this mild melancholia, I have slowly realized again
how much I love my life. On my desk sits
a portrait of my father, and even after twenty years
I am shocked to think I will never see him again.
Tears well up in my eyes and they are beautiful,
welcome, their crystal liquid filled like a crystal ball
with the streets of sorrow, streets of hope, streets of blues
and whores and jazz, streets down the end of which
great friends live, down the end of which
live lovers you have not met, down the end of which
there is no end after all. Hello, dad. Your inheritance
is this burden that I'll lay down only once
when I step into the dark street of forever
and turn around and around
until I finally find your eyes and tell you
Thank you. Thank you. Thank you. Thank you.